SCREWED

By

KENDALL RYAN

D1501243

About the Book

I have one rule: Don't shit where you eat.

Several of the women in the condo complex I own would love some one-on-one playtime, and why wouldn't they? I'm young, fit, attractive, and loaded. Not to mention I'm packing a sizable bulge below the belt. It's a combination that drops panties on a regular basis. Yay, me, right?

But my cock, troublemaker that he is, has been confined to my trousers by my business partner. A concession I agreed to, and one that's never been hard to enforce until Emery moves in across the hall. She's smart, young, determined, and sexy as hell. I want a taste. I won't stop until I'm buried deep inside the succulent new-in-town brunette.

After being warned about my past, she does her best to steer clear, but I'm about to show her that underneath it all, I'm a guy with a heart of gold and a cock of steel.

My name is Hayden Oliver, and this is my story.

Chapter One

Hayden

Goddamn. This is going to be harder than I thought.

My eyes swing over to admire the most perfect pear-shaped ass I've ever had the pleasure of laying eyes on while my business partner, Hudson, continues lecturing me. I think it's about something important, but there's nothing more urgent than my body's reaction to this shapely brunette. *Jesus.* Those tits are definitely real.

"I mean it. Your cock is cut off this time," Hudson says, his tone biting.

Tearing my gaze away from the succulent new brunette moving into unit 4B, I face him. "Not literally cut off. I'm sort of attached to him. You realize that, right?"

"Well, it's on lockdown then. No more of this bullshit. I had three calls this week alone from hysterical women—our tenants who you, how do I put this delicately? You fucked and then left before their pussies were even dry."

I smirk at him, but I can't deny the accusation. The condo building that Hudson and I own—and I live in—is like a real-life Melrose Place. With sexy young twenty-somethings all living in close proximity, there's bound to be a little drama now and again. Together, Hudson and I own thirty buildings in the greater Los Angeles area. And some of our buildings have very fuckable tenants. Up until this point, I've considered that a nice bonus, a bonus that I accepted numerous times; it was certainly the best perk of the job. Hudson has apparently viewed it differently.

"Who's that?" I ask, tipping my head toward the bombshell who's responsible for all the blood rushing to my groin. *Fuck.* I should have a word with her about that; that's not cool. But the thought of going up to her and having a word about my current predicament and seeing her blush causes my groin to ache even harder. *Fuck.*

Hudson's eyes swing to the left to see what, or rather, *who* has captured my attention. And who's given me this semi-chub, which I hope he hasn't noticed. We're close, but we're not *that* close.

"Get control of your cock," Hudson says, narrowing his eyes at me.

Damn it. He noticed.

"The only one I want in control of my cock is that beautiful creature right there." I'm blatantly staring at her, and I don't even care.

"No, no, no. Don't get any ideas. You're not tagging that."

She's not close enough to overhear us, but I shoot him a scowl anyway. "Show some class, man. Tagging is such a juvenile word. I'd take my time, get her hot and ready first, until she was begging for me to fill her tight little cunt."

"I'm fucking serious. You're not to even think about her tight cunt." He puffs his chest out, clearly ready for battle.

"So you acknowledge she's got a tight cunt?" I smile, proud of myself.

He wipes sweat from his brow, looking worried.

"Hayden, I'm serious this time." His voice has taken on a somber tone, and for once, I try to be serious and focus.

When I see the way the vein throbs in his neck, my smile fades. We're standing outside one of our nicest buildings just outside of downtown, and the mid-afternoon sun is beating down on us. Suddenly I want to get away from him, away from this entire conversation and into the cool air-conditioning inside. Shit has gotten a little too real for me.

"You know me." I grin at him, trying to lighten the mood. "I just wanted to have some casual fun." And if that means sleeping my way through the LA singles scene, so be it.

I'm not looking for something deeper. I have a luxury condo in the heart of the Hollywood Hills, drive a new BMW, and possess a nine-inch cock. Translation: Life is good. Or it was, until Hudson decided to get a bug up his ass and lay down the law today.

"Did you hear a word I just said? One of your latest conquests threatened to report our company to the Better Business Bureau for unethical business practices.

This isn't just about you. This affects me too. And I'll be damned if I watch everything we've built go down in flames because you can't keep your dick in your pants."

"Point taken."

Hudson is pretty much the best friend and best business partner you could ask for. He's smart as hell and dedicated, works like a dog day and night. And not to mention when we began our real-estate investment company five years ago, he singlehandedly fronted all the startup capital from his own savings and trust fund. It took me years to pay him back as the profits rolled in, and he never once made me feel lesser, or like I was in debt to him. Not to mention, he's funny, well-off, and good-looking. He's an excellent wingman. Plus he knows how to find the best tacos. And I'm not talking about the kind served with salsa. The dude is a magnet for pussy.

Unable to help myself, I allow my eyes to drift over to her again. The woman moving into 4B fills out a pair of yoga pants in ways that I doubt are even legal in some countries. I need to know what's underneath those curve-hugging black athletic pants. Simple cotton panties, or a naughty G-string? Either way, I want to bury my fingers inside the waistband of those pants, peel them down her hips, and find out. Perhaps it's because Hudson just made her forbidden fruit, but I want a taste. My damn mouth is practically watering.

She looks smart and put together, despite her casual attire that includes a tank top and tennis shoes. With a clipboard in one hand and her trusty number-two pencil in the other, she ticks items off her list, and instructs the movers who are unloading and carrying boxes up to her new place—which just so happens to be directly underneath mine.

"You're not going to last three minutes, let alone three days." Hudson grimaces, glancing over again at our newest resident.

"What do you know about her?"

He rolls his eyes but humors me. "Emery Elaine Winters. She's an attorney. Excellent references. Even better credit score, and she signed a one-year lease. And she, and her pussy, are to remain in pristine condition, or so help me God . . ."

I can't help the inappropriate comment just hanging on the tip of my tongue. "I could make sure her engine is running properly, give her a tune-up, if necessary."

Hudson growls out a curse.

When I glance up at her again, I see Roxy, another of our residents, has joined Emery on the sidewalk. They appear to be making small talk, shaking hands, exchanging words, and smiling at each other. There's something I strongly dislike about these two women talking. Roxy is an exotic dancer, and she and I have a bit of a rocky past. Which is a huge fucking understatement, but not something I care to dwell on now. Hudson mentions something about fourth-quarter taxes, and I tune him out, sure I just heard my name on Roxy's over-glossed lips.

"Excuse me, I've got business to attend to." I step around him, heading straight toward my new prize. Roxy spots me and takes off for the parking area.

"Where do you think you're going?" Hudson calls after me.

"Just being neighborly. Someone's got to properly welcome Miss Winters."

"Damn it, Hayden," I hear him shout.

"I've got this, buddy," I shout back over my shoulder.

I can control myself around her. I have to, according to Hudson. I don't like being told what to do, especially where my cock is concerned, and hell, it'll probably only make me want her more. But as I close the distance between Emery and me, I make a plan.

Friends.

I will become friends with the *so hot I want to bend her over and fuck her in broad daylight* new girl.

This is either the best plan I've ever had, or will end with me sporting a black eye, courtesy of my best friend.

It's go time.

Chapter Two

Emery

The blazing sun beats down on me, causing little beads of sweat to form at the back of my neck. My hand is damp where I'm holding the clipboard, and I wipe my forehead with my other arm. I feel a little ridiculous, sweating like a pig while I'm just directing the movers, who are doing all the actual work.

I'd known that Los Angeles would be hot, especially in June, but nothing could have prepared me for this. To a born-and-bred Michigan girl, "shorts weather" is pretty much anything above freezing. A hundred degrees might as well have been a million, for all it meant to me. Seeing a number on a weather report is completely different from feeling it in the flesh. I lick my chapped lips for the umpteenth time—the humidity, or lack thereof, is yet another thing I have to get used to.

"Hey there!" calls a bubbly female voice. "You look like you could use this."

I turn to see a tall, dirty-blond woman holding out a bottle of water. I swallow at the sight of the cold droplets beading along the plastic. "Oh . . . thank you." I accept it and drink fast. Before I know it, the bottle is half-empty.

She cocks her head with a slight smile. "You're new to these parts, right?"

"How could you tell? The lack of tan?" I look down at my fish-belly white arms that sharply contrast with this woman's perfectly bronzed skin. My skin is already starting to turn pink with the first hints of sunburn. *Damn it.* I thought I put on enough sunscreen.

"I was going to say you still look bright-eyed and hopeful. Plus you weren't carrying your own water." She holds out her hand. Her nails are deep scarlet, perfectly manicured, and way too long to be real. "I'm Roxy. Looks like we'll be neighbors—I'm in unit 3C."

I shake her hand firmly. "I'm Emery. Unit 4B."

Now that I'm not ready to die of thirst anymore, I can get a good look at my new acquaintance. She has legs all the way from her ass to the floor, as my mother would say, although her stiletto sandals made me think that she's taller than she really is. She's wearing Daisy Dukes and a blue halter top that defies the laws of physics to contain her huge fake breasts. She's also wearing enough makeup to spackle a wall—heavy foundation and bright blush, shimmery hot-pink lip gloss, a lush forest of false lashes, and plucked and penciled brows arching high over turquoise-shadowed eyes.

Overall, not the kind of person I'd usually pal around with. But she seems sweet. And in my sweat-soaked tank top, yoga pants, and tennis shoes, it's not like I'm exactly dressed for success either.

"So, what brings you to the city of angels?" she asks. "Looking to make it big in Hollywood?"

"Actually, I have a summer internship at a law firm downtown. I start on Monday." That's as much as she needs to know. I didn't uproot my whole life and move across the country to dwell on the past. I want to put my shiny new diploma to use, dive headfirst into my career—and leave a certain douchebag in the dust.

"Oh, wow! I could never do a high-powered job like

that . . . way too much stress. I work long enough hours as it is." Her dark brown gaze drifts over my shoulder, and her expression suddenly sours. "Ugh. Don't look now, but . . ."

Of course, I look now. Over by the outdoor stairwell, two men in dress shirts and creased suits are talking. They're both attractive, and one of them keeps stealing glances at us.

He seems around my age, maybe a year or two older. He's ridiculously handsome with an angular jaw that has just the right amount of stubble, and a ready smirk that begs to be either slapped or kissed. His short dark hair is cut just long enough to grab onto, although why I'd need to grab onto it, I'm not sure. His broad shoulders and trim waist hint at some very nice muscles beneath his business attire. Even beyond his surface-level hotness, there's something strangely magnetic about him, something that makes my stomach twist pleasantly just looking at him. Something that makes his slightest movement scream *sex*.

Feeling hot for reasons that have nothing to do with the actual temperature, I quickly turn back to Roxy before the man can notice my stare. "Who are those guys?"

"That's Hudson Stone and Hayden Oliver. They're the real-estate investors who own this building . . . a lot of buildings around here, actually."

For real? They both look so young. Someone must have a rich daddy. I resist the urge to look over again.

"What's so bad about them? Do they screw people over on rent or something?"

Roxy shakes her head. "Nah, everything that's on paper is fine. These places are more than worth what you pay for them."

God, I hope so. My new luxury condo is probably the biggest splurge I've ever made. Sometimes I still feel guilty about dropping that much cash, even if it is a good deal for a location in Hollywood Hills. But I figured that I deserve a treat after surviving law school on top of my latest breakup. Besides, if I'm going to walk the big-city lawyer walk, I should also talk the talk. "Dress for the job you want" doesn't just apply to clothes, right?

I realize that Roxy has continued on without me.

" . . . and Hudson is a pretty nice guy. He's polite when he comes around, which isn't often. But Hayden is the landlord here, and it's him you want to watch out for. He's fucked his way through half the single women in the city, even some of his own tenants. Treats his properties like an all-you-can-eat buffet. What a shameless piece of shit. And he lives upstairs in 5B, so nobody can get away from him without moving out."

Her story feels like a bucket of ice water straight down my panties. A checkered past like that would kill anyone's buzz, no matter how attractive the son of a bitch is. I've had enough of men who can't keep it in their pants to last me a lifetime. Besides, I'm here to succeed, not sleep with my new landlord—or with anybody, for that matter.

I tamp down what's left of my libido and nod at Roxy. "Good to know. Thanks for the warning."

She gives her hand a breezy flip. "No prob, sweetie. Us girls gotta look out for each other, right?"

"Hey, lady," a burly moving guy says, interrupting us.

He's standing next to us with a medium-sized box under his arm. His eyes aren't focused even remotely near our faces. "What room you want this in?"

With my pencil, I point at the huge capital letters written in black marker on the side of the box. "The label says 'bathroom,' so it goes in the bathroom. Anywhere is fine." I cross my arms over my cleavage and raise my eyebrows, letting him know he's been caught. "The next time you want to get a closer peek at a woman's chest, try to come up with a better excuse."

He gives me a serious dirty look. But I just stare up at him as coolly as possible until he wanders off again.

Roxy chuckles behind her hand. "I think that's my cue. I'll let you get done moving in, but you should totally come over for a glass of wine sometime. Or we can do lunch. Have some girl talk."

"Sure, that sounds nice," I reply with a smile. And it really does. I don't know anyone in this big, strange city, so I sure could use a friend.

She waves as she walks away, then disappears toward

the parking lot.

Hopefully I'll actually have time to hang out with her. In law school, I was no stranger to eighty-hour weeks, and my professors all said that practicing law in the real world is even more grueling. But I know I can take whatever this internship throws at me. Bring it the fuck on, I say silently.

I go back to checking off items on my clipboard and directing the movers. Despite the butterflies in my stomach whenever I think about my new life, I'm not looking forward to the long, grimy weekend of unpacking boxes that lies ahead of me. And then I have to get settled into my job, knuckle down on studying for my bar exam next month . . .

Footsteps approach, quiet crunches on the asphalt. I look up to see Hayden The Playboy standing right in front of me.

Chapter Three

Hayden

My first thought is that she's not from around here. Her skin is pale and creamy, not bronzed with the golden tan most of us natives maintain year-round without any effort. Long dark hair hangs down her back, and she pushes it out of the way as she takes another look at the clipboard she's holding.

I can't help but introduce myself, even though there's no purpose for it. I merely own the building; I'm not involved in the day-to-day of running it. If Emery needs help or has questions about her new condo, she'll work with our building manager in the office just around the corner.

The truth is I just wanted to see those curves up close. And holy hell, the view just gets better the closer I get.

That firm, round ass needs a good spanking for making my dick so hard. Generously sized tits, smooth and shapely shoulders, and now that I can really see her features, my gaze focuses on her face. A small, pert nose, high cheekbones, full lips, and thick black eyelashes that rest on her cheeks as she looks down. I tower over her petite frame, but nothing about her is diminutive. I suspect there's a robust self-confidence just beneath the surface. Her shoulders are pulled back, and she stands tall and proud. I notice that she doesn't have any problem telling that moving guy to keep his eyes off her tits. *My kind of woman.*

As if sensing my presence, Emery glances up when I get near. Her eyes are captivating, two wide-set pools of blue filled with curiosity. She's a deep thinker. A thoughtful girl, if my hunches are correct.

"You're new here," I say, my tone confident and direct as I treat her to full-on eye contact. Women love that shit. And I couldn't look away right now, even if I wanted to. *Jesus, she's pretty.* Like *spring an awkward erection and come way too soon* pretty. I'm in deep shit here. Momentarily speechless, I tuck my hands into my pockets and wait for her to respond.

"What gave me away?"

I expect a friendly smile or at least a sly grin, but Emery is watching me with a wary expression and guarded eyes. Her tone is flat and emotionless. *Damn, that stings more than it should.*

Extending one hand toward her, I attempt a warm smile. "I'm Hayden Oliver. I own the building, and I live upstairs. I just wanted to introduce myself and see if you needed anything."

"I'm Emery. And I'm a little busy, if you'll excuse me." She looks down at her clipboard once again.

No way, sweetheart. You're not getting rid of me that easily.

I hold up both hands, my smile widening. "I'm harmless."

"That's not what Roxy said." Emery looks up at me as she says this with no warmth in her features.

That's what I was afraid of. "I'm a pussycat. I promise." I treat her to a wink, and Emery dissolves into a fit of laughter. It's not the reaction I was expecting.

"I'm sorry." She holds up a hand while trying to get

herself under control. One more hiccup and she's there. Lowering her hand, she grins at me. "Do lines like that actually work for you?"

Ignoring her question, I attempt to regain the upper hand. "Where are you moving from?"

"Michigan. I just graduated from law school, and I have an internship at Walker, Price, and Pratt. I start on Monday."

"I heard you were a lawyer."

She shakes her head, and there's a faraway look in her eyes, as if she's thinking about something unpleasant. "I'm not a lawyer. Not yet. I'm a legal intern for the summer."

I nod. Even a blind man could see this job opportunity is important to her. She's moved across the country for it, and I'm guessing she has to prove herself this summer to be hired on full-time.

"Walker, Price, and Pratt . . . that's downtown, right? Near Pershing Square?"

She nods. "I think so. At least that's what Google Maps

said."

I nod. "It's not hard to find. And there's a great sandwich shop within walking distance. It's called Louie's Lunch Shack. Just avoid the tuna salad, and you'll be golden."

I'd made the mistake of ordering that once. Never again. I shudder just thinking about it. I spent the next twenty-four hours in the bathroom, and my good buddy Hudson had to play nursemaid, restoring me back to health.

"Thanks for the tip."

"Anytime. That's what I'm here for." What am I here for? Why am I standing here talking to this beautiful woman who I know I can't have?

She just stands there on the sidewalk in the bright sunlight, as if she's waiting to see what I'll do next. I've never felt quite so unsure of myself. If Hudson hadn't just given me a verbal lashing, I would have her upstairs in my condo with her panties around her ankles by now.

"We should grab a drink later, when you're done

moving in," I say. I'm hoping she's ready to call it a day now. It's almost the weekend, and it's five o'clock somewhere. Maybe alcohol will smooth over this tension between us.

She chews on her lower lip, thinking it over. "I really can't. I'm sorry."

Taking a step closer, I lean in toward her. "Is this about something Roxy said?" *Fucking Roxy.*

Her gaze skitters away from mine, and lands on the moving truck where the men lifting boxes grunt and scurry off for the elevator. "It's not that, it's just I'm here to focus this summer. I've just come off a bad breakup, and I'm *so* not looking for anything."

"What did she say?" My tone comes out more commanding than I intended.

"Roxy?" she asks.

I nod.

Emery chews on her lower lip again. "That you're a dirty, dirty man-whore who's had his fair share of fun. And then some."

"True on all accounts." No use in denying it. I don't like liars, and so I make it a habit never to be one myself.

Emery gazes up at me. *Damn*. Those eyes. It's like they see straight through me.

"If liking pussy is a crime, lock me up. I'm as guilty as they come. I like the taste of it, I like the smell of it, and I especially like the way it feels when—"

She holds up her hand, her cheeks turning bright pink. "Do not finish that statement, Mr. Oliver. I get the point."

Shit. Have I just been rambling on about how much I love pussy? I need to get ahold of myself.

I glance up at her. Her pulse has quickened in her throat, and her face is flushed. She gives me a look that women normally only give when they want to drop to their knees and service me. Or is there something in her eye?

My dick leaps to life.

Her gaze drops to the front of my pants. "I have a big

dick ahead of me," she says, and her cheeks flame bright red. "I mean a big day. *Day*," she repeats.

"Are you okay?" I ask as she shakes away that massive Freudian slip.

She swallows and gulps down a deep inhale of air. "I'm fine."

"Listen." The urge to reach out and take her hand, to physically connect us in some way, surges through me. But I press on. "I'm not looking for a hookup. I didn't mean to insinuate anything. Honestly. We could go out—strictly as friends—and I could show you around. You're new to the area. I could help. That's all I meant."

I remind myself: *Friends only. I can do this. I can prove Hudson wrong.*

She presses her lips together, and I'm assuming she's about to shoot me down when she sighs again.

Chapter Four

Emery

Hayden comes trotting over almost the instant Roxy leaves.

Why do I suddenly feel all tingly? No. That isn't part of the plan. He does not get to strut over here and make me go all lusty for his dirty, dirty man rod. Especially after what Roxy just told me. Has my vagina no shame? There are probably cooties crawling up and down that overused flagpole.

I blame my body's indecent reaction on the current state of my love life. Which is sucktastic, thanks to my dipshit ex essentially ruining my trust in mankind.

As I watch that sexy beast of a man head straight for me like a cheetah approaches a gazelle, I give myself a mental pep talk. The plan is to keep my head down and work my ass off so that my aging mom can finally retire, and not fall for a cheating, lying asshole ever again.

Period.

When he flashes me that gorgeous grin and asks me out, I'm unprepared, but I do my best to fend off his suggestive comments.

He keeps trying to charm me despite my clipboard, my short, bored responses, and my best bitch face. I'm absolutely not in the mood to fend off a *won't take no for an answer* guy right now.

But at the same time . . . dear God in heaven, he's even more handsome up close. How does that work? Isn't closeness supposed to ruin the illusion? I guess he traded all his external flaws for internal ones. Or his cologne is some secret mind-control weapon; the smoky spice makes my mouth water, makes me wonder if he tastes anything like he smells. And it's been so damn long since I've had sex—let alone *decent* sex.

Even remembering all the horrible things Roxy just told me, I still feel a little flip deep inside when he grins at me. And when he leans closer, I can't even look him in the eyes. Which are a beautiful shade of blue with a hazel starburst in the middle.

Somehow I doubt his offer is just a "friend date" like he claims. Rambling about pussy kind of undermines that argument. But maybe letting him show me around Los Angeles won't be so bad. It's probably best to start off on the right foot with him. After all, he's this building's owner, its landlord, and my upstairs neighbor.

That doesn't mean I'm ever going to sleep with him—God, of course not. I'm just being polite. Politely ignoring the way he's already made a total ass of himself. That's how classy I am. Winning friends, influencing people, all that jazz.

As I'm weighing my options, he watches me as if he's never had to wait this long before. Finally I reply, "Okay."

There's that thousand-watt grin again. "Terrific. Just wait . . . I'll show you where to get the best steak in town."

"I'm a vegetarian," I fire back. When he merely blinks, I smile at him, feeling slightly evil. Just because I'm playing nice doesn't mean I have to go easy on him. Not right away, at least.

"Fair enough." He rubs his chin. "Then I'll take you to the beach. I know some spots with great views where we can avoid the tourists."

I shrug, shaking my head. "I'm not really a beach person. Too many bugs and too much sand in unmentionable places." Now I'm just having fun with him. Poor guy, he didn't know what he was in for with me.

To his credit, he refrains from commenting on my unmentionable places. I'm guessing that takes serious restraint on his part. "Seriously? You moved to Los Angeles and you're not a beach person? That's like someone moving to Colorado when they hate skiing."

My mouth presses into a firm line. "Or like someone moving to Colorado for work and not for goofing off."

Hayden pauses to brainstorm another date idea. I wonder if other women ever make him work for attention like this. No, with other women, I'm guessing all he has to say is: *You. My bed. Now.* And they shimmy out of their panties and sprint to his bed. I'm not—and have never been—one of those women. Even if my body's response to him is more primal than I would like.

Out of the corner of my eye, I notice that the rental truck is empty and the movers are toting my last few boxes up the stairs. It's time for me to see them off. I paid their fee in advance, so all I have to do now is order dinner, find the box with my pajamas, and call it an early night. I walk over to the stairwell, forcing Hayden to follow me if he wants to finish our conversation.

"Fine. Then what *do* you like to do?" he finally asks.

I think for a moment as I start climbing. Most of my life is work, study, sleep, then rinse and repeat. Well, that and I drink copious amounts of wine. But something tells me sharing a bottle of pinot with this dangerously sexy creature would be a bad idea with a capital *B*. But there is one thing I do to unwind . . . and I'm curious about how he'll respond.

"I like yoga," I say. *These pants ain't just for show.*

He hesitates, which doesn't surprise me. What I hadn't expected was for him to say, "Sure, I could do yoga. When's good for you?"

Say what now? It doesn't sound like he enjoys yoga, or even that he's ever done it before. But hey, that's no skin off my nose. If he wants to try it on for size, I could always use a workout buddy.

"I'm going to be busy unpacking all day tomorrow, so how about the day after? Meet me outside my unit at, say, six?"

"Six in the morning?" He says *morning* in the same tone that I might say, "Is that blood?"

I look over and bite back a smile, feeling evil again at the faint look of horror on Hayden's face. "Of course," I chirp as brightly as possible. "Yoga works best when you do it before breakfast. Gives you energy for the whole day." *Unless you're not up for it?* I add inside my head.

But smooth as silk, he replies, "Sounds great." He steps ahead and opens the door to the fourth-floor hallway for me, playing the gentleman. "I have to get back to my office now, but I'll see you on Sunday."

Stunned, I step inside, almost sighing aloud at the frigid wash of air-conditioning. Without thinking, I say,

"Looking forward to it," then realize that I actually mean it.

Hayden waves good-bye and trots back downstairs. I follow the hall to unit 4B, thank the last few movers on their way out, and lock up behind them. Then I turn and lean against my front door, savoring the quiet. I'm finally alone in my luxury condo. My new home— hopefully for years to come, if I pass my bar exam and play my cards right at Walker, Price, and Pratt.

Even cluttered with dusty boxes, this place is gorgeous. The furniture is sleek and stylish, but comfortable. All the countertops are granite; all the tables are glass-topped. Although there are only two real rooms, they both feel huge compared to the apartment I shared with three roommates in law school. The kitchen is fully loaded and offers enough room for a dining area. The other half of the unit has a queen-sized bed, a walk-in closet with mirrored sliding doors, and a fifty-inch flat-screen smart TV mounted on the wall above the foot of the bed. Best of all, the porcelain bathtub is long enough to lie down in without concussing myself on the toilet.

I kick off my tennis shoes, feeling the cool hardwood floor on my hot, tired feet, and stow them in the entry closet. On the other side of the front door is a tiny table, just large enough for a glass key dish and a china vase holding three purple tulips. I gently stroke their velvety petals to confirm that the flowers are indeed real. Then I weave through the stacks of cardboard and slide open the door to my biggest indulgence: the small balcony.

Even when splurging, my guilty conscience has its limits. I chose a studio model rather than a one-bedroom, and I only ponied up for a furnished unit because it was cheaper than shipping my own furniture over two thousand miles. But the prospect of a balcony—of basking in the sun while I read, sipping wine on breezy evenings, enjoying what feels to me like year-round summer—had been just too tempting. I go outside and drink in the view of swaying palm trees, mansions with blue-green lawns, and Lake Hollywood sparkling in the distance. If I squint, I can even glimpse the blocky white letters of the Hollywood sign.

I spend almost half an hour just strolling around and inspecting the entire unit. Of course, I knew exactly what it looked like before mailing in my signed contract and down payment. I pored over the property management website, admiring the photo gallery, the floor plans, and the long list of amenities. But now is the first time I'm seeing it in person. All elegant and cozy. All mine.

Once again, the difference between anticipation and reality hits me—and not just with the condo itself. My landlord isn't quite what I imagined based on Roxy's description. But he hasn't disproved any of that scathing story, either. It'll take a lot to make me relax my guard with him.

Still . . . if Hayden actually shows up on Sunday, I think I just found a new yoga partner in my building's man-whore owner.

This should be interesting.

Chapter Five

Hayden

Why in the fuck did I agree to this?

I swing my legs over the side of the bed, cursing at myself for this brilliant fucking plan I hatched with Emery—the girl in 4B—who I'm most decidedly *not* banging. That's bullshit right there. I should be waking up with my cock in her mouth, not because I told her we'd do yoga this morning.

Yoga, for fuck's sake.

It's not the best plan I've ever had, especially after the amount of Jack I downed last night. My head is spinning like a top as I grab my phone and dial Beth's number. I know she'll be up at this ungodly hour.

"Beth. Help me?" I croak once she answers.

"What did you do now, you fuckwad?"

"Jeez. Is that any way to talk to your favorite brother?" I cradle my phone between my shoulder and chin and head into the kitchen to fire up my espresso machine. *Make it a double.* Why in the fuck had I thought it was a good idea to drink so much last night? Oh yeah, because Hudson laid out all my demons, examining each one in the harsh light.

"You're my *only* brother. Now get on with it. I have yogurt smeared into my couch, and I haven't had my coffee yet."

I should ask why her kids are allowed to bring yogurt into the living room, but I know from past experience that she lets those rug rats get away with anything, so long as they bat their little eyelashes at her. My niece and nephew are three and four years old. To say they're a handful would be a huge underestimation of their abilities.

Instead I rub a hand through my sleep-styled hair and lean my hip against the counter. "Do you know of a good yoga place I can take my friend Emery this morning?"

"Friend?" she asks, choking on the word.

I grit my teeth and hit the BREW button on the machine. "Yeah, she's new in town."

Several moments of silence follow. If it weren't for the two little voices arguing in the background, I might have thought she hung up on me. "Beth?"

"Yeah. I'm here. Sorry, just a little flabbergasted."

"About?" I roll my eyes, knowing what's coming.

"You have a *female* friend, and you're taking her to *yoga*." She enunciates each word in a tone of pure disbelief.

Precious drops of dark liquid drop into my waiting mug and I consider, briefly, licking them out rather than waiting for the cup to finish brewing.

"Yes. Why?" My tone is short, but shit—after Hudson's pep talk, Beth's attitude is pissing me off. Doesn't anyone believe I can keep my dick in my pants? It only makes me want to prove them all wrong.

"Well, for starters, you don't have female friends, and secondly, you don't do yoga. Forgive me for being completely caught off guard here. Who are you and what have you done with my brother? Plus, why are you up so early?"

"I could do yoga," I say, my male pride wounded. *It can't be that hard, can it?*

"Of course you can, it's a free country. I'm just confused. Are you feeling okay? Are you sick?"

My headache intensifying, I take a deep breath. "Will you help me or not?" All humor is gone from my tone. I didn't expect a fight when I called her this morning. I called needing answers, not to play Twenty Questions. I knew Beth's mommy friends did yoga, and I knew she wouldn't steer me wrong. If she could focus long enough to give me the damn information.

"Take her to Deep Connections on Sepulveda."

The name of the studio sends my thoughts spiraling— about just how *deeply* I'd like to *connect* with my new neighbor Emery—preferably my cock in her warm cunt. *Mmm . . .*

"Hayden, did you hear me?"

"Yeah. I've got it. Thanks, sis."

"I'm on their website. There's a class starting in forty minutes. Now, I want to hear more about this Emery." I can hear the smile in her voice.

"She's a lawyer." *Almost. Sort of.*

"Wow. A girl with brains. That's a nice change of pace for you. Tell me about her."

Smirking at the memory of meeting Miss Succulent New-in-Town Brunette, I grab my cup of espresso. "I thought you had a yogurt situation to take care of."

"What? No. That can wait."

It's then I notice that her kids have gone completely silent. Either that or she's locked herself in the bathroom, hoping for some privacy while she grills me for details about my private life. *Ding, ding, ding.* That's the much more likely scenario.

My gut instinct is to blow Beth off, to tell her it's none of her business. But as I stride across my living room and sink into my favorite leather armchair, I realize that would be a dick move. Even though she's annoying at times, Beth and I are super close. Despite being my older sister, she's also one of my closest friends. I eat dinner with her family a few times a week. When she needed an emergency C-section with her second baby, I was the one who moved into her guest room for two weeks to help take care of her and the baby after her husband, David, returned to work. And she's always been there for me no matter the favor, big or small.

"Hayden, stop holding out on me. There's got to be a story here. Spill it."

I chuckle at her desperation before taking another sip of my scalding-hot beverage. "There is. And I'll tell it to you."

"But not right now?" she says, the hope in her voice fading.

"If I'm going to make it to that class, I've got to go meet Emery." Glancing at the clock, I see it's already almost six.

"Fine. Dinner Tuesday night?"

"Of course. Will you make those little crab roll-up things with the sweet chili sauce?" I ask in the kindest voice I can muster.

"No one likes those but you," she says with a sigh. She sounds tired, and hell, I would be too after chasing around two mini humans all day, hell-bent on destroying everything in their wake. Damn, I shudder just thinking about it.

"No, you don't have to bother, then. Forget I asked, and I'll see you on Tuesday."

"Have fun at yoga," she says, a teasing lilt to her voice.

Despite the caffeine coursing through my veins, I don't feel any better than I did when I woke up this morning, grumpy and hung-the-fuck-over.

Heading into my bedroom, I step inside the walk-in closet, trying to figure out what one wears to do yoga. I settle on a pair of loose-fitting navy athletic shorts and a gray T-shirt. After brushing my teeth, I grab my wallet, keys, and cell phone where they're resting on the kitchen island, and head out into the bright sunshine of yet another perfect day in LA.

I grunt the whole way down the stairs, wondering why in the fuck I agreed to this—hell, I practically insisted on it. I'm grumpy. I'm pissed off. And as I knock on

Emery's door, I stand there seething and silently cursing at myself.

When it opens, Emery's waiting there, looking delicious in a formfitting pair of black leggings and a pink tank top, and I remember exactly why I invited her out today. *Hello there, inappropriate boner. Nice timing, dickhead.*

"Are you ready?" I ask, my voice thankfully sounding calm in a way that doesn't match the way I feel when she's near.

"You actually showed." She treats me to a smile. Her lips are full and natural, without any gloss or lipstick, and her teeth are straight and white.

"Of course I did." Placing one hand against the door frame, I lean in close. I catch notes of citrus and something floral on her skin. She smells freshly showered, and good enough to eat. "I'm a man of my word. You may have heard some unsavory stories about me, but don't you think you should decide for yourself?"

She lifts her chin, meeting my gaze head-on. "I always

decide for myself." Then she bends down to pick up what I assume is a yoga mat—it's rolled into a neat cylinder—and a bottle of water, before closing and locking her door.

"Let's go. I have just the place." I help Emery into my BMW while she shoots me curious glances.

She buckles her seatbelt and tucks her hands in her lap before turning to face me. "Why are you doing this?"

As the engine roars to life, all 445 turbocharged horses, I say, "Just relax, okay. I'm not going to try and get into your panties, if that's what you're worried about."

"You're not?" She sounds almost offended, and I can't help but smirk.

"Not unless you ask very, very nicely." And that's the honest-to-God truth. For me to betray Hudson like that, she'd have to be literally begging for it. I don't think I could stop myself if that were the case.

"It's good to know the option's there." She smirks back at me, and I can't tell if she's joking or serious. She's unlike any lawyer I've ever met before, and I like that.

"What kind of law do you practice?" I ask as I drive.

"M&A," she says, staring straight ahead as though she's trying to take in every detail of the palm-tree-lined boulevard we're cruising down.

I give her a blank stare as my fuzzy brain tries and fails to make meaning of those two letters.

"Mergers and acquisitions," she says, helping me out.

"Ah. The good ole M&A. What do you enjoy about it?"

She thinks for a moment, those wide blue eyes never straying over to mine as she watches the landscape change when the Santa Monica Mountains come into view. "I like the challenge of getting the best deal I can for my client. Mostly I like the fun of negotiating and winning. I've never been very good at sharing—I was an only child—and I think it's served me well in this field so far. I work hard and I play to win." She smiles, and I want to kiss that grin right off her face.

"You said you're just an intern this summer . . . ," I say, encouraging her to tell me more. For some reason, I like hearing her talk. With most women, I'd be happy to sit in peaceful silence without having to listen to their incessant chatter.

Emery's not like that at all. When she speaks, it's because she has something to contribute. I've always liked that Gandhi quote: "Speak only if it improves upon the silence." And in this moment, I understand what he's saying. Hearing her talk, learning about her and what makes her tick, it's fascinating. It most definitely improves on the silence.

"Yes, it's not uncommon for the top students in law school to be offered positions before they've passed the bar. I take my exams later this summer."

"So basically, you have to pass a test to keep your job?"

She nods. "It's three days of tests, and yeah. No pressure, right?"

Suddenly I admire her even more. She's set a lofty goal for herself, moved across the country, and has to prove herself to just keep her job.

"Are you from around here?" she asks, turning the topic away from herself.

"Born and raised. My parents live up north now, but I have an older sister who lives in the valley, and a younger sister who lives downtown. I attended UCLA, and after graduating, I saw no point in moving from a state with near-perfect weather and plenty of opportunity. Plus it's great working every day with my best friend, Hudson."

She nods. "It sounds perfect."

I chuckle. "It's not. Trust me. But I enjoy it, and like you, I work hard, and play even harder."

She turns toward me, treating me to a warm smile just as we reach our destination.

I like how things are already so comfortable between us. It's unexpected, and while she keeps me guessing about what will come out of her mouth next, I'm certainly not bored.

"You ready to get your yoga on?" I ask, parking the car near the studio's entrance.

Emery steals glances over at the unimposing building. "Deep Connections," she says, reading the sign hanging above the door. "I'm ready if you are."

I shrug. I'm game for an adventure. How difficult can yoga be? Isn't it just breathing and stretching?

I soon find out no, no it is not. Fuck, I'm going to kill my sister. After we paid our fee and enter the studio, I find out that we've signed up for Advanced Hatha Techniques III.

The instructor asks the class if everyone has completed the level-two course, and there are nods all around the room, while Emery and I share an apprehensive look. I'm about to try to talk her into leaving with me. A big plate of eggs and pancakes and a cup of coffee sounds way better than doing god-knows-what for the next sixty minutes. But she unrolls her mat and looks ready to do this.

Around the room there are more than a dozen people, but they're all women—believe me, I checked. There are twenty-four boobs in this room, plus the female instructor, so that makes twenty-six and only one cock. Usually that would be like unleashing a kid in a candy store, but instead I feel like a fish out of water.

The instructor begins in a warm, almost saccharine tone. "Raise your arms above your head, lengthen your spine, and allow your body to prepare for this beautiful journey we'll take together this morning."

Seriously?

I look over at Emery, and her eyes are closed. She's standing tall, her bare feet on the yoga mat and a small smile gracing her lips. I think I've just discovered her happy place.

As we begin, I push my body into the warrior pose, sun salutations, and downward dog. There should be a special place in hell reserved for the person in charge of coming up with these names. For instance—the plow pose—that's nothing like what I would have assumed it would be. At the very least, it should be done with a partner.

I can't help my gaze from straying over to Emery every so often. She's flawless with her poses, graceful and elegant as her body seamlessly transitions from one pose to the next. I'm intensely attracted to her. But remembering my vow to Hudson, I tamp down the feelings of lust stirring in my gut.

Maybe this morning's yoga will give me a new outlook on life. I will prove to myself, Hudson, and Emery that I can keep it in my pants and have a meaningful platonic relationship with a woman.

Even as my thoughts wonder, my body continues attempting the poses. I can't even imagine how I must look. I'm not flexible or graceful, and would rather be in the weight room or jogging on the beach.

At last, the class is done. Emery's practically glowing; she looks so content and at peace.

"What did you think?" she asks, bending down to roll up her mat once the instructor has dismissed us with a "Namaste."

I could pull some alpha-male attitude and tell her that men shouldn't twist into those positions, but instead I offer her my hand and smile. "It was cool."

She grins widely. "Really? You'd do it again?"

"Let's not get ahead of ourselves." Next thing I know, she'll be trying to get me to go to Jazzercise or Zumba.

And I'm not about to turn in my man card. No fucking way.

She chuckles and we head from the studio with a light sheen of sweat over our skin, and feeling energized.

"Oh. They have wheatgrass shots there. And fresh juices." Emery's voice is excited as she stops in front of the small café at the front of the building. "You want anything?" she asks.

I shrug. "Sure."

I discover that *juice* is a relative term. Because theirs are green, and brown and chunky. I order a bottle of water while Emery gets a little glass of something green and downs it quickly.

We find a table in the café, and sit down. I continue sipping from my water bottle, trying to rehydrate.

"Thanks for bringing me here today," she says.

"Of course."

As we sit here, chatting about mundane things like the disgusting wheatgrass she's currently drinking, I realize that we challenge each other. She keeps me on my toes.

"Tell me more about you," Emery asks, leaning in toward me.

"What do you want to know?"

"Enlighten me." She shrugs.

Leaning back in my seat, I cross my ankles. "My job is pretty much my life, and I love what I do. Taking an old run-down building and turning it into luxury units that rent for top dollar is awesome. It never gets old. I love seeing the transformations."

"That's amazing." She nods. "What else . . . surely there has to be more to you than just work."

"You want to know something deep, huh?"

She nods, eager.

I think about it for a second, and memories of my checkered past flash through my brain. But rather than watch her expression turn to one of sympathy when she learns of my past, I'd rather see her face light up with a smile. "Blow jobs are my spirit animal."

She rolls her eyes at me, but laughs.

Mission accomplished.

"You seem normal enough. What in the hell did you do to piss off Roxy?" She chuckles as she says this, and suddenly all the blood in my veins turns to ice water.

I scrub a hand across the back of my neck. "Roxy and I . . . it's a long story, and not one I care to discuss right now."

She pouts. "Fine. Regardless of your history with Roxy, you didn't deny what she told me about you."

"What exactly did she say?" Now I'm actually curious.

She shrugs, playing with the long strands of hair from her ponytail that rest on her shoulder. "She just warned me to stay away from you. Told me about your man-whore background."

"Well, your virtue is safe. I made a deal with my business partner. No more sleeping with tenants." I'm not sure why I'm telling her this, maybe because it'll be easier to enforce the friends-only rule I've set for myself if she knows that she's off-limits to me.

"So sleeping around in general is still fine?" There's a mocking tone to her voice.

"Absolutely. This will be just friends." I gesture between us. "Unless, you naughty girl, you're trying to tempt me." I give her a flirty wink.

She frowns and shakes her head. "Not a chance in hell. I told you. I'm done with men, and you, Hayden Oliver, by all accounts are a piece of shit."

"Excuse me?" I cock an eyebrow at her.

"I've dated guys like you before. And I classify all men who think with their dicks under *S* for *Shitty*."

"I do think with my cock on a regular basis, so I can't argue with you there. But he's so much more fun than my brain."

This gets a small smile from her, and my heart beats just a little faster.

"Seriously, why would I take a chance on you and have my heart broken again?"

"Because I have a nine-inch cock and I know where the G-spot is?"

Her cheeks turn pink, belying her cool, confident tone. "Tempting, but not good enough."

I shrug. "Then I guess I'll settle for just being friends."

"Do you even have any women friends?"

I think it over. I have Dottie and Susan, but they're more employees than friends, and of course Beth and Gracie, but they're my sisters, and I doubt blood relatives count. "Of course I do," I lie.

She narrows her eyes, obviously on to me. Nothing gets by Emery. She's going to be a kick-ass attorney. Of course I don't tell her that. Her self-esteem is robust enough. She doesn't need me overinflating her ego.

"Just relax, princess. I won't try to get in your panties unless you ask nicely, and I'm serious about the friends thing. I'll show you around town. It'll be fun."

Her mouth presses into a line, but she doesn't say anything else.

Our bantering has left me with a half hard-on I'm trying to conceal under the table. Emery doesn't need to know that I'd like to fuck her six ways from Sunday until she's clenching around my cock and screaming out my name.

Chapter Six

Emery

Monday morning at seven thirty sharp: the first day of the rest of my life.

I stride into the law office of Walker, Price, and Pratt, refreshed after my usual morning workout and a Greek yogurt smoothie for breakfast. I feel sleek and confident in my long black pencil skirt and matching blazer, powder-blue buttoned shirt, and sky-high nude pumps. I spent almost two hours yesterday obsessing over my wardrobe and makeup, wanting to make a professional first impression, and I think I've nailed it. Even if my walk from the parking lot was a race against time and tottering on my barely manageable heels.

I approach the sleek wraparound marble desk in the lobby's corner, and take a deep breath. *Here we go.* The receptionist looks much younger than I would have predicted, maybe even around my age. Her thick black hair is pulled back tight in a ponytail to avoid tangling in her headset. She wears tortoiseshell cat-eye glasses, a loose rose-colored pullover blouse, and khaki slacks, which makes me wonder if I should have wasted so much time and energy on my own outfit. Her plum-painted fingernails fly over the keyboard, tackity-tacking like a train rattling over railroad tracks.

It takes her a moment to realize I'm standing there before she looks up from her work. "Can I help you?" she asks with a plastic smile.

"Hi, I'm Emery Winters. Is Mr. Pratt here yet?" He's the partner I had corresponded with the most, but if he hasn't arrived yet, I can still talk to the others and get started. *The joys of a workplace where every other employee is your superior.*

There is no spark of recognition whatsoever in the receptionist's green eyes. "Do you have an appointment?"

I chuckle; someone has dropped the ball here, and it clearly wasn't her. "In a way. I'm the new summer intern."

Genuine pleasure enters her smile. "Oh, I'm so sorry,"

she says, her happy tone at odds with her words. Maybe she's relieved that her duties will be shared with someone else now. "I'll call to tell Mr. Pratt you're here. I'm Trina, by the way. Would you like any coffee or water while you wait?"

"No, thank you. I can grab something after I get started." *After all, I work here now.*

The thought fills my stomach with butterflies. *Calm down, Emery, this isn't summer camp. I'll be fine.*

I consider one of the caramel-colored leather chairs, then decide I'm too nervous to sit down. Instead I watch Trina buzz the senior partner's office, then announce, "There's a Miss Winters here to see you," in a singsong voice before she resumes her furious typing.

After a minute or two, a man walks in from the hallway to the left of the reception desk. He looks like he's in his early sixties and desperately trying to cover that fact up: iron-gray hair, a slight paunch, skin like tanned leather, and a neatly brushed mustache. Glossy brown wingtips and an olive shirt with black suspenders complete the picture of a man who was hot shit about thirty years ago. But there's no ring on his left hand, making me wonder if he's divorced, a "confirmed bachelor," or just really unlucky.

As the man comes closer, he gives me a toothy grin that shows off thousands of dollars in dental veneers. "You must be Miss Emery Winters. Welcome to Walker, Price, and Pratt."

I smile back at him, hoping there's no lipstick on my teeth, and extend my hand. "Good morning, Mr. Pratt. It's great to finally meet you in person."

He gives my hand two firm pumps, a textbook handshake, the greeting of someone who knows how to charm and intimidate without saying a word. "Please, call me Larry. I don't like to stand on ceremony in this office."

Somehow I'm not sure whether to believe that. Powerful men, especially if they're old and rich, like people to *perceive* them as laid-back—but when it comes to how they actually prefer to be treated, most of them want deference. At the same time, though, I can't just blatantly ignore what he said. "Okay, then . . . Larry."

He looks me up and down, still holding my hand. "My, my. I knew from your phone interview that you had a lovely voice, but the rest of you is even more so."

Say what? I blink at him, trying to figure out how to respond, and quickly decide to pretend he said something else entirely. "Um, I'm glad my attire is appropriate for the office."

"A little too appropriate, if you ask me."

I can feel his eyes surveying me up and down, and when they settle on my chest, I have to look to make sure I didn't miss a button on my blouse.

Larry continues with an amused tone. "You'll find that California is much more casual than the Midwest, even in our line of work. Let loose, have a little fun . . . I certainly won't mind." He winks and I try not to let my lip curl in disgust.

"Thank you. I'll keep that in mind," I say in a carefully neutral tone. In deference to the mindboggling heat, I may take this excuse to ditch my blazer tomorrow, but I'll be damned if I give this guy any more of a show than he's already getting.

Just when I'm starting to wonder if I'll have to rip my hand away, he finally releases it. "Before you get started, honey, I'd like to show you around the office. Meet our other lawyers, get acquainted." He turns toward the hall entrance and I start to scurry after him . . .

Only for his hand to fall securely on my lower back, just a couple of inches above my ass.

Oh, hell no. I suppress a full-body shudder.

Mr. Pratt steers me like a show dog through the hallways, stopping to knock at each door. The two "junior" partners are both in their fifties; Mr. Walker is round and balding, while Mr. Price has salt-and-pepper hair and impressive jowls. They both glance away from their laptop screens, cough out a distracted "pleasure to meet you" without getting up, and go right back to work. The four associate lawyers—Misters Ingersoll, Morton, Kemp, and Mendoza—are only slightly younger and more gracious. It's exactly the sausage-fest that I expected.

Lucky for me, it's also clear that my new coworkers are

way too busy to care whether I'm a young woman, yet another old fart, or a flying purple people-eater. All they see is an extra set of helping hands. That attitude may become a pain in the ass if I ever need something from them. But for now, them aggressively minding their own business is downright refreshing, compared to Mr. "please call me Larry" Pratt and his creepy wandering hand. He obviously wants to bury his face in something *other* than his work.

Finally our tour is over and we end up back in the lobby. "Last but not least, my dear," Mr. Pratt announces, "this will be your office." He points to a narrow whitewashed door, across the hallway entrance from the reception desk, that I had assumed led to a broom closet.

My eyes widen. Holy shit, I get my own office? With a door and a desk and everything?

"Normally we have two or three interns who share that room, but for now, you'll have the place to yourself. Don't hesitate to knock on my door if you get lonesome." His leering grin kills any excitement I may have felt at my new private domain.

"I'll be sure to come by if I have any questions," I say, forcing my face to stay blank. Translation: I'll only talk to you if everyone else in the office has suffered a gruesome death. *Maybe I'm the only intern because the other ones gnawed off their legs to get away.*

His hand finally leaves my back, only to land on my shoulder like a giant leech. "I promise I'll let you get to work now. But I want to take you out to lunch today. Just the two of us, so we can get to know each other. I like to know all my employees . . . especially the ones who are as pretty as you."

Over his shoulder, I see Trina stand up and start frantically cutting her hand at her neck, giving me the universal gesture for ABORT! Her eyes are wide and her mouth is pulled down in an exaggerated grimace of horror.

I quickly look back at Larry before he follows my gaze. "Uh . . . you know, I'd love to, but I brought my lunch today. I mean, I always bring my lunch. Saves money."

"You can put your lunch in the fridge and save it for tomorrow. Don't worry about the money—this is my treat, sweetheart."

One more minute with him and my skin is going to crawl right off. Would *that* get him to leave me alone, or would he just compliment my bone structure?

"I actually already told Trina that we'd eat together," I blurt. Thank God she said her name earlier, or this lie would be even more unbelievable than it already is. "We were going to talk about . . . you know, girl stuff."
Babies. Boys. Makeup. I have a tampon in my purse and I'm not afraid to use it.

Mr. Pratt frowns, looking annoyed and confused. But all he says is, "Well, that's too bad. Let me know if you're ever in the mood for male company."

I nod solemnly at him. *No, it isn't too bad. It's the best thing ever.*

With one last damp squeeze of my shoulder, the slimy creature finally retreats to its lair. Trina waves me over to the reception desk as soon as his office door clicks shut. Now that she's on her feet, I realize that she's freaking tiny. I am by no means tall, but she stands maybe five foot one, even in her heeled sandals.

"Sorry if that was weird," Trina says softly. "I figured you wouldn't want his hand on your knee for a whole goddamn hour. And even if he insists on paying, it's always a trap. Turn him down and he acts like you're the rude one, but if you let him spend money on you, he starts thinking it's a down payment, if you know what I mean. Obviously, you should start packing your lunch for real, but for today, you can share mine. Gives me an excuse to buy chocolate out of the vending machine later. I hope you like linguine with garlic sauce and feta cheese . . . stinky breath will keep him out of your face. It's a real life-hack."

My head is spinning with Trina's mile-a-minute diatribe. What the hell have I gotten myself into? I moved here to work hard and become a successful lawyer, not to fend off dirty old men all day.

"This isn't a situation you should need to life-hack," I finally sputter. "You . . . *we* have the right to do our jobs without having to jump through all these stupid hoops. Creating a hostile work environment is illegal."

She shrugs, turning her palms up. "All very true. But what are you gonna do about it? There's nobody to complain to when the big boss is the rotten one."

And such a small company wouldn't have a human resources department. Or even any real legal protection against employee sexual harassment. Still . . . "There must be something we can do. This is fucking ridiculous."

"You *can* do plenty. Whether you *should* is another question. The last intern who told him to knock it off got fired. Hell, that's probably why my job opened up two years ago. So unless you want to jump straight to taking him to court—"

"And probably lose the case. And then still get fired. Okay, I get the picture." I rub my forehead hard between thumb and finger.

Is every man in this city total scum? So far, Trina's the second friend I've made through the *watching out for each other* clause of the Girl Code. My boss may be even worse than my landlord. I didn't think that was possible, but at least Hayden isn't twice my age and has the common sense to keep his hands off me. Is being valued for my brains instead of my breasts really so much to ask?

I force myself to take a deep breath and set my jaw. I refuse to let yet another man's bullshit ruin my life. I refuse to waste all the time and money and effort I've already invested in this job. Everything from shot-gunning my internship application at a hundred law firms to blowing thousands of dollars on moving to Los Angeles—and even further back, all the sacrifices that Mom made to send me to the best schools. This is my big break, and by God, I'm going to grab it with both hands.

I expected this internship to be mostly busy-work and acting as a gofer, especially in the first few weeks. But when I finally get down to business on day one, I'm pleasantly surprised to find myself drafting briefs, indexing files, and doing research instead of fetching coffee and making copies.

In the few moments when he wasn't sleazing all over me, Mr. Pratt mentioned something about a huge corporate M&A case; evidently the other lawyers are so busy handling it that they're forced to delegate. I'll probably learn the details about that case at the next meeting. Right now, I'm thrilled to be treated more like a paralegal than an errand girl. Intellectual challenge is the entire reason I studied law in the first place. And as a bonus, I can cloister myself in my tiny, quiet office like a monk in his cell and avoid Larry The Creeper without too much trouble. If he wants to pester me, he has to knock.

Around noon, someone does come rapping, rapping at my chamber door. I brace myself for annoyance, but it's only Trina asking if I want lunch yet. I invite her in and we chat while sharing her pasta. Mr. Pratt never bothered to introduce me to Trina, but he damn well should have. It turns out that she pulls double duty as the firm's legal secretary as well as its receptionist. Anything that needs to get done around here will probably pass through her hands at some point. And we have a lot in common; she's studying for her paralegal certification, just like I'm studying for the bar. In an office dominated by old men, she's a fun, irreverent breath of fresh air.

But as much as I enjoy lunch with Trina, my mountain of paperwork soon starts calling my name again—and it doesn't stop calling.

I arrive home that night at eleven thirty, exhausted but still exhilarated. When I step inside, my foot lands on something that makes a crinkling sound. I look down to see a pile of takeout menus that have been slipped under my door. The topmost one has a note attached.

Thought you might need these when you're burning the midnight oil—Hayden.

Still standing in the threshold, I leaf through the menus. Almost a dozen local restaurants are represented here, and they're all vegetarian-friendly: Indian, Indonesian, Chinese Buddhist, Ethiopian, Egyptian, Mexican, and Italian, even one called Veg-Love Café. Somehow I doubt he had that just lying around. There's the predictable but reliable soup-and-salad bar, and a cute little place that sells nothing except crepes, both sweet and savory. There's even an American-style burger joint specializing in black-bean-and-quinoa patties.

My heart melts a little. Hayden must have spent quite

some time putting these together.

Before I can talk myself out of it, I lock up again and climb the stairs to unit 5B.

I knock on Hayden's door, smoothing my skirt with my other hand. I probably look like a total wreck after a fourteen-hour day. I should have checked in my bathroom mirror before I came up here. Wait, never mind . . . it doesn't matter. I don't care what he thinks of my face. Really, I don't. We're just friends, after all.

The sound of his doorknob turning jerks me back to attention—and for a moment, all I can do is stare. *What am I doing here again?*

Hayden has no shirt on. What he does have is full, firm biceps, a washboard stomach, and perfectly squeezable pecs dusted lightly with hair. His loose gray sweatpants hang low on his lean hips, showing a dark happy trail. Is that bulge my imagination, or was he really not lying about having a nine-inch cock? Jesus, what would it look like when it's hard?

"Emery? Earth to Emery?"

I realize I've been ogling him like a horny schoolgirl and blurt out the first thing I can think of. "Wow, you're up late."

"So are you," he replies, holding up a glass of amber alcohol on the rocks. He's smirking. God damn him, he's mocking me. The last thing the world needed was for me to feed his ego. "I was just having a nightcap. Want to join me?"

Definitely. Wait, no. Bad girl. No boner for you. "Thanks for offering, but I've had a really long day. I should get to bed soon . . ."

"All alone?"

I snort, though I'm smiling despite myself. "Yes, alone. You know, for sleeping? Some people have work in the morning." Although I may be willing to lose a little more sleep for some quality time with a battery-powered friend, if only to get myself under control. "I just came up here to thank you for the menus. That was really sweet of you."

He gives a nod, blue eyes crinkling in a boyish grin that shows his dimples. And this smile isn't just a show to dazzle my panties off, though it threatens to do just that. It seems genuine—as if he's pleased that he pleased me.

"No problem. What with your crazy hours, I figured you wouldn't have much time to cook." He pauses for dramatic effect. Or could he be hesitating? "Would you be interested in going to one of those places sometime? You know, in person. Without any plastic sporks."

"Oh, I don't know . . . real plates and silverware?" I sigh in mock wistfulness. "Sounds too rich for my blood."

"Come on. You're going to be busting serious ass. Even if you can't take an early night during the week, you deserve some fun on the weekend."

I consider for a minute. I usually work weekends too, but Hayden's offer actually sounds pretty tempting. After my first week of a new job, it may be nice to unwind with someone to talk to. I can brag about all the Real Lawyer Stuff that I'd never expected to do as a lowly intern. I can vent about Creepy Larry. If he was this bad on the first day, I can only imagine what kind of bullshit he'll pull in the future.

Finally I nod. Stealing an hour or two for dinner won't hurt much. "Okay, you win. I'll take a break with you. How about five thirty on Saturday, at . . . the burger place I'm totally blanking on?"

"You mean Sunflower Grill? Sure thing. As long as I don't have to say that name ever again, and they sell something that tastes like meat."

I roll my eyes. "Yeah, yeah. The caveman never shuts up about his meat." *In more ways than one.*

His smirk should be disgusting, but it just draws my attention to his soft lips. "You don't like my meat?"

"Good night," I call out, already walking away with every ounce of nonchalance I can muster.

Glancing over my shoulder, I find him still watching me, and a warm tingle rushes down my spine. I go back downstairs to my condo, take a very quick, very cold shower, and fall asleep with a stupid smile on my face.

For the rest of that week, in the moments between pounding out work and taking my short lunch breaks with Trina, I find myself thinking fondly of Hayden. I'm looking forward to our non-date more than I probably should.

Chapter Seven

Hayden

This place is an absolute zoo, which is no surprise. Beth's finishing up in the kitchen while I set the table. My niece and nephew are in the living room, arguing about which show to watch on the iPad, and my brother-in-law, David, is due home any minute.

Beth carries a platter of baked chicken into the dining room and sets it in the center of the table. "You want a beer or something?"

"Only if you join me."

She gives me a sarcastic smirk. "Anything for you."

When she returns, she wrangles both kids into their booster seats and sets their plates in front of them. Then she hands me a bottle of beer and a little plate of those crab roll-up things she usually only makes for special occasions or holidays.

"You're my favorite sister," I say, stuffing one into my

mouth.

"Love you too." She smiles.

"This *almost* makes up for you sending me to an advanced yoga class." I look at her and frown.

She smiles, and the twinkle in her eye tells me that was quite intentional on her part. *Brat.*

When she encourages me to sit, I take in the table filled with steaming bowls of veggies, potatoes, and a platter of chicken. She rocks at this mom thing.

"Should we wait for David?" I ask before popping another of the roll-ups into my mouth.

She shakes her head. "He'll be home any minute. He said to start without him."

We're digging into our food, making small talk about what's new with the kids, when David comes strolling in moments later.

He leans down to give his wife and children each a kiss before greeting me. "How've you been, Hayden?"

"Good," I say. "Come on, food's getting cold."

For being a guy who's fucking my sister, he's actually pretty cool. They've been married seven years and are good together. He joins us, sitting at the head of the table. If it weren't for their generosity, I'd eat takeout most nights of the week. Instead, I come here.

After dinner, David and the kids play in the driveway while Beth and I tackle the dishes. I used to try to encourage her to go out and play, let me handle the work, until I realized that she'd been playing with them all day and actually just wanted some adult conversation. Now I happily supply that.

We have a system. She passes me plates, and I rinse and stick them in the dishwasher. Only tonight, she uses our sibling time to grill me.

"So . . . Emery. Yoga. You owe me details, little bro."

"That's what those crab roll-ups were about. Damn, you're good."

She grins an evil smile at me. "Don't mess with the master."

I chuckle. "She just moved in last weekend. She's from Michigan and is working at a law firm downtown." I fill her in on my experience at yoga, and before I know it, I realize I've been prattling on about Emery for ten minutes. I've only stopped short of describing the fabulous way she smells and her glorious rack.

I can't help but remember how cute she looked after her first day of work. Rumpled suit, killer heels, and little makeup smudges underneath her eyes. She'd put in a hard day's work and was obviously tired, but there was still that undeniable spark of excitement simmering just under the surface that I'd grown to appreciate about her. I still wonder what might have happened if she'd said yes and taken me up on my offer for a drink.

"Wow. I'm impressed," Beth says, taking a break from wiping down the counter with a dish towel to face me. "Are you finally going to settle down and date a nice girl? She sounds sweet and normal."

"No, come on. We've had this conversation before. I'm not looking for anything serious."

She tosses the towel into a basket in the pantry. "God,

what's wrong with you? This girl sounds great. Why not just see where it goes?"

"Because, Beth, not everyone wants a house in the suburbs with two kids. It wasn't the life I was meant for." Not anymore, anyway. Not after what happened with Roxy. But I do my best to push that from my head.

"Right, because emergency trips to the clinic when your pee-pee burns are so much fun."

I square off, facing her with an angry scowl. "That was one damn time, and it turned out to be nothing. And you've been hanging out with toddlers too much. It's called a cock."

"On that note, I have to get them ready for their bedtime routine."

Beth heads for the back door, and I reach out and stop her. "Hey. I didn't come here to fight with you. Just let me live my life my way, okay?"

There's fire in her eyes, and she puts one hand on her hip. "You've never dated your emotional and intellectual equal. You always go for these *one night is good enough* girls who jump into bed with you on the first date. They don't have goals. They don't have careers. And surprise . . . they don't hold your interest longer than one night."

"First of all, I'm not *dating* anyone. And second, what's wrong with one night? I have needs, you know."

She rolls her eyes. "Oh, I know. I shared a bedroom wall with you in high school, remember?"

"Where is this coming from all of a sudden?" I'm trying to understand, because up until this point, sure, she's occasionally given me shit for my lifestyle, but it's always been with a mocking laugh in her voice, a jab to the ribs while she grins at me. Right now she seems legitimately pissed off.

"You were top of your class in high school, graduated early and with honors in college. It makes sense that you should be with a smart, capable woman you can have lively discussions with, someone to hold your interest and challenge you."

It's strange that she uses that word—challenge me. Isn't that exactly what Emery did? Making me go to yoga, asking me to explain my past. Refusing my offer for a late-night drink.

"Who's going to take care of you when you get old, Hayden? I want you to have a partner in this life. God, I picture you sixty years old with a bad fake tan and dyed hair, still trying to live this playboy lifestyle. It's sad."

"I'm only twenty-seven, Beth. Calm down."

"Yeah, well, you're going to blink your eyes and tomorrow you'll be thirty, and all the good, quality girls will be married. I'm only trying to look out for you."

"I know you are. But just try and relax, okay? Everything will be fine."

She lets out a heavy exhale. "I just don't think you can do it, being friends with a woman. Be careful with this one."

Her lack of faith in me feels like a kick to the balls. Beth's always been my biggest cheerleader, supported me in every crazy thing I wanted to try.

"I'm going to go. Kiss the kids good night for me."

She nods, her face solemn.

• • •

On the drive home, I can't keep my thoughts from replaying Beth's angry words and her condescending tone. I tighten my grip on the steering wheel and try to focus on the road. The sun is just beginning its descent for the evening, casting a hopeful ambient light on everything. I grab my cell and press the contact I call most often.

"Hey, dude. What's up?" Hudson answers after a couple of rings. "You got an update on Summer's Edge?"

We just spoke a couple of hours ago about a poorly performing apartment complex called Summer's Edge we're trying to offload onto another investor. It's in a decent area of town, but the complex itself is comprised of older units that rent for cheap. There always seem to be several vacancies and unpredictable tenants, which doesn't help when you need steady cash flow to plan your business. It's also going to need a new roof and an overhaul to the heating and cooling system within the next two to three years. If we can sell it for the right price before then, Hudson and I won't have to deal with the headache of owning Summer's Edge anymore, something we're both very much looking forward to.

"No. No updates yet," I tell him. "I'm guessing we'll hear back from the investor sometime tomorrow." Without taking a breath, I add, "Beth doesn't think I can have a female friend."

He pauses for a few seconds, as if trying to catch up to the abrupt topic change. "That's bullshit. You can do anything you set your mind to. I've seen it."

Hudson, only a couple of months older than me, has always been infinitely wiser.

"Thank you," I say, feeling the tiniest bit redeemed. "I've sort of struck up a friendship with the newest tenant, Emery. Beth was giving me shit about it."

Several moments of stony silence follow, where I'm sure Hudson is trying to process what I've just told him.

"Well, don't torture yourself. Just because I've laid down the law on not hunting in the herd doesn't mean you can't get laid. You can be friends with Emery. You'll just have to go back to hitting the bar scene again to hunt for pussy."

Why does that idea hold zero appeal? Standing around in a too-loud bar, buying drinks for girls who I know after one glance will let me walk them outside and fuck them in the back of my BMW. The idea just doesn't excite me like it used to.

"Yeah, of course." Suddenly I don't know why I've called him. "Update me if you hear anything from the investor."

"Will do, buddy. Have a good night," Hudson says, ending the call.

As I pull into my usual parking spot, I can't help but look up at Emery's front window. It's dark, and I wonder if she's still at work. The idea depresses me on her behalf. No one should have to work that hard. I'll do everything in my power to make sure she has fun when we go out to eat this weekend.

Not too much fun, though. The kind of fun where my cock stays neatly tucked into my slacks. *Oh, joy.*

Chapter Eight

Emery

On Friday evening, I walk to Rico's Taquería with a plan to scarf down dinner in twenty minutes and hightail it back to work. But as soon as I sit down with a cold beer and a hot quesadilla, the fatigue of my first week suddenly all comes crashing down on me. I must have been running on pure adrenaline for a while now. The office was almost deserted when I left, anyway, so I decide to call it an early day and head home. After polishing off the huge quesadilla and a beer, I'm more than ready for the weekend.

I've just taken off my shoes when someone knocks on my condo door. I open up to see Roxy. Her outfit tonight is even more memorable than the one I first saw her in. Tonight she's wearing a skin-tight leopard-print minidress with side cutouts and matching platform stilettos.

She gives me a little wave. "Hey, girl," she sings. "Want to hang out sometime? I meant to ask you sooner, but this past week has been nuts. Desiree got food poisoning, so Angelique and I had to take over her shifts."

Still feeling loose and carefree from a good time with Hayden, I answer on impulse. "Is now a good time? I'm not doing anything." The night is still young, after all. Even if I can barely translate legalese right now, I have enough energy and focus for casual chatting. A little girl talk sounds like fun.

Roxy raises her penciled eyebrows in pleasant surprise. "Awesome. Wait a sec, I'll bring over a bottle of wine. You like red or white?"

I shrug. "Whatever is fine."

She leaves and comes back in a few minutes with a big bottle of local Shiraz. As she sets it down on the dining table, she asks, "Mind if I smoke?"

"Um . . ." I look around my fresh-smelling, pale-carpeted place. "Let's sit on the balcony."

We grab two wineglasses and a corkscrew and go outside. The moon is almost full; the stars twinkling invisibly in the sky are reflected in the city lights below us. I pour the wine while Roxy lights up.

The night is calm and she tries to exhale away from me, but sometimes a gentle breeze still catches her smoke and makes me splutter a little. The smell is faintly nostalgic. Dad used to sit out on the porch and smoke a pipe in the evenings. Although he was gone by the time I was two years old—and even though the smoking probably helped kill him—the scent of tobacco sometimes reminds me of Mom's stories. She always talks so affectionately about him, it's like he just stepped out for a moment.

Roxy takes a long drag and sighs it out in feathery white tendrils. "So how's the Golden Coast treatin' ya?"

I start recounting my first week in Los Angeles. Mostly my shiny new job, since I'm still starstruck about working for an actual law firm, and I've done almost nothing *but* work since I got here. Not that I mind practically living at the office.

I'll probably repeat most of this stuff to Hayden over dinner tomorrow, minus the goriest details about Larry The Creeper. It's stupid, and I know it's stupid, but I

still feel embarrassed about how I let my boss treat me
. . . and how I intend to let him continue treating me, all
for the sake of keeping my job. I don't know what
would be worse—Hayden failing to see what the big
deal is about Mr. Pratt's behavior, or Hayden
demanding to know where he lives so he can kill him in
his sleep.

So it's nice to talk to a woman who can really
commiserate about the problem without trying to play
Mr. Fix-It. Roxy cackles and grimaces in all the right
spots of my stories. As good a friend as Hayden is
becoming, there are some things that most men just
don't understand.

"I think changing my outfit helped a little," I say as I
finish. "Flats instead of heels, pink lip gloss instead of
red lipstick, dress pants instead of a skirt. And a
camisole under my blouse to make sure there's no
cleavage showing." Not that Mr. Pratt hasn't looked for
it. He practically broke his neck trying to see down my
collar at the Wednesday lunch meeting.

"So has he stopped touching your ass and acting like it's
an accident?"

"No, but he does it less often. Although he's started dropping all these passive-aggressive comments, like 'Where's the funeral, har de har?' or 'Oh, you looked so sweet before, what happened?' Or my personal favorite, 'You don't need to dress like a nun, sweetheart. You should enjoy that amazing figure while it lasts.' So I consider it a mini victory."

"What a douchebag." Roxy rolls her eyes. "I've had gross customers before, but I knew what I was getting into when I started working at Kitty Queen's. You didn't bust your hump in college just to put up with some old perv. And strip joints have a bouncer who can step in if someone gets too rowdy. At your job, you're on your own. Worse than on your own, actually, since the problem is with the guy who's supposed to protect you. Not that I haven't had a few handsy bosses before . . ."

When she first told me she was a stripper, I barely batted an eyelash. Once you meet her, it seems the most obvious profession in the world for her. She's outgoing, gorgeous, and confident, with just a hint of being a wild child. The only thing that surprised me was that she didn't use a more subdued euphemism, like dancer or exotic entertainer or something. Then again, there's nothing subdued about Roxy.

I swallow my mouthful of wine. It isn't great—not far from the realm of two-buck Chuck—but it's loosened me up just fine. "Sometimes I think you can never win with men," I add.

"Words of goddamn wisdom." Roxy gives a huff of acrid laughter, smoke pouring from her nose. It reminds me of the femme fatale from some noir film. Or a dragon wearing expensive lingerie.

Wow, I think I'm getting a little drunk. Maybe that's why I suddenly feel the urge to talk about Hayden. "Sometimes they aren't so bad, though."

"You mean for decoration? Boys do make great accessories." She nods, her chandelier earrings bouncing.

"No, I mean . . . I've been hanging out with Hayden, and he's actually pretty cool. We do yoga together almost every morning now. And tomorrow, he's going to a vegetarian restaurant with me, even though he's clearly a meat-and-potatoes kind of guy." I realize that a silly little smile is pulling at the corners of my mouth. It's so odd. When I hang out with him, I have a mysterious sort of glow for the rest of the day. He makes me laugh, and heaven knows I could use a good laugh with the seriousness of my job.

"It's great that he hasn't screwed you over yet," Roxy says, her tone abruptly tense. "But he's still bad news. Ask any of the girls here."

"He's been a perfect gentleman so far." Well, not perfect, but good enough for government work. "We're just workout buddies."

"You think he's your friend? Sorry to burst your bubble, hon, but he doesn't bother with women for anything other than the obvious. He's working for a reward that starts with 'p' and ends with 'ussy.' Get out while you still can."

Once again, I wonder where all this barely suppressed rage is coming from. But mostly I'm annoyed. Roxy is talking down to me like I'm some naive country girl who doesn't know her ass from third base. I've met my share of shitty men, thank you very much, and I like to think I can see them coming by now. I'm old enough to make my own decisions and smart enough not to get in over my head. Plus, for once in my life, I want to do something really impractical—like own a convertible in Seattle. I want to say *fuck it* and just have fun.

"I know he's a player," I say, a little more testily than I intended. "I knew that when I started hanging out with him. A guy doesn't have to be perfect if all I'm after is a casual friend. It's not like we're getting married—it's just nice to have someone to eat with sometimes."

That's part of the reason why Hayden can be so refreshing. Neither of us has to be perfect. We don't even have to *act* perfect. We aren't putting on performances or evaluating each other. We can just enjoy the good parts of each other's personalities and not bother stressing over the bad parts.

At the same time, though, a little voice in my head whispers, *Maybe Roxy is right.* I can't help but remember how obviously Hayden was lying when he said that he had female friends. Both the truth and the fact that he lied about it are potential bad signs.

I try to ignore that nagging voice as I finish my point. "I'm not under the delusion that my magic vagina will cure his no-good womanizin' ways. I just escaped Boyfriend Hell; I won't go back to see if it's frozen over since the last time I checked. I'm on a no-man diet until further notice. So if Hayden *does* try to get into my pants, I'll tell him he's barking up the wrong tree, and he can either stay one hundred percent platonic or fuck off." I look up at Roxy with close attention. "Unless you're trying to tell me to look out for roofies in my drink?"

"No, no . . . Hayden's nothing like that." She drops her cigarette butt and grinds it into a small blackened blotch with the pointed toe of her shoe. "He's purely small-time. More than bad enough to make you feel sorry for yourself afterward, but not enough for anyone *else* to feel sorry for you."

More and more questions are jostling into my head, so I choose one of the least nosy ones. "If he's so horrible, then why do you live in his building?"

Her fuchsia-painted lips tighten into a line. "I'd already lived here for years when Hayden bought it. The fact that he ended up being my landlord is total coincidence."

"So move out and find a better place."

An even harder edge enters the set of her mouth. Pure bitter stubbornness. "Why should I be punished for his B.S.? I was here first, and I'm not going anywhere when I didn't do anything wrong. It'll take a lot more than one annoying asshole to push me out of my own home."

Okay, okay, I think, nodding at her a few times. *Defensive much?*

My impression of the real Hayden is nothing like what Roxy said when I first moved in. Sure, he's a horn-dog and he seems kind of immature, but he's fun, and I can't deny his eye-candy appeal. I almost giggle when I remember him trying to get into the downward dog position. What harm could there be in just hanging out with him? Is his laid-back playfulness really nothing but a Jekyll-and-Hyde act, lulling me into a false sense of security? Or could Roxy just be overreacting?

When I asked Hayden for the dirt on him and Roxy, he

flat-out refused to go into it, which just makes my imagination run wild. Is Roxy the villain of that story, I wonder, or is Hayden? I try to dismiss the thought. Real life is rarely so cut-and-dried.

But my curiosity about what relationship they had is still driving me nuts. Roxy is so insistent that Hayden doesn't "do" friendships with women, so if they ever *were* friends, Hayden must have let his lust get in the way somehow.

Are they ex-lovers? For all I know, she could be his sister. I kind of hope so. For some reason, the thought of Hayden sleeping with this woman bothers me, even though his sex life is none of my business. Even though I shouldn't care whether or not Roxy, with her inflatable boobs and pancake makeup and a beach body way nicer than mine, is his "type." Because if she is, I most definitely am not—with my closet full of suits and no-nonsense bras and panties.

I put down my wineglass, shaking my head. What's wrong with me? Just thinking of Roxy like that makes me feel like a huge bitch. She went out of her way to befriend the new girl on the block, came over here to share wine she bought with her own hard-earned money—which she probably had to pick out of her butt crack after a long night of dancing—and here I am being catty.

Other women are not the enemy, I remind myself. But I can't shake this territorial feeling. Hearing her badmouth Hayden pisses me off, and not just because it implies that I'm too dumb to realize I'm walking into a trap.

Screw it. At the risk of opening a can of worms, I ask, "So, just what is your deal with Hayden, anyway? What happened to make you hate him so much?" If Hayden won't satisfy my curiosity, maybe Roxy will be interested in dishing dirt. She certainly seems to have strong feelings in need of venting.

She goes very still, her hand halfway to tapping another cigarette out of its pack. I already regret my question a little; mixed in with Roxy's expression of loathing, I catch a glimpse of something dark, like grief. Or maybe it's shame.

Finally she mutters, "We used to date. Beyond that, let's just say he made a mistake and tried to dump the consequences on me."

So they *were* lovers. She must have been one of Hayden's many one-night stands. Just another conquest. I sit back, taking a long drink of wine while I try to think of a response. Roxy's vague answer hasn't really cleared up anything, and I feel bad for asking her in the first place.

In the end, I can't think of anything to say other than, "I'm sorry that happened to you."

"Worry about yourself, sweetie . . . I'm just trying to protect you." Roxy reaches out to squeeze my shoulder, careful not to jab me with her talons. Her dark, glitter-shadowed eyes are deadly serious. "I don't want to see another girl get hurt by that tool. He's a man-child and he'll drag you down with him. He's the center of the fucking universe—all that matters is what he wants, and to hell with everyone else. You're a smart girl on your way to a great career. Don't let him distract you. Don't let him weasel in between you and what you want out of life. Don't let him convince you that his shit is more important than yours. And he'll try, believe me. He has a way of talking up into down and black into white.

Women do what he wants while thinking it was all their own idea."

At a loss, I nod soberly at her. "Okay." It's not a promise to take her words to heart; it's not agreeing with anything. Just an acknowledgment that I've heard her.

She and I finish the bottle of wine in silence. I still think she's being paranoid. Whatever happened between her and Hayden, it poisoned the well pretty damn good. But where did that contamination come from in the first place? From her or from him? Sometimes breakups are nobody's fault at all. Without hearing the whole story, there's no way for me to know how much weight to give Roxy's warning. Even a first-year law student knows how much personal bias can distort a testimony.

I shake my head with a wry sigh; I'm already thinking about this in terms of depositions, evidence, and judgment. I should just unplug my brain entirely, turn the conversation to lighter things, and enjoy my impromptu night off. And tomorrow, I may even ask Hayden when we can hang out again.

I'm not going to stay away from my friend just because his bitter ex told me to. I'm a grown-ass woman; I can handle myself, even with a guy like him.

But I still can't uproot the tiny seed of doubt that Roxy has planted.

Chapter Nine

Hayden

It's five thirty on Saturday, just like we agreed, when I tromp down the stairs toward Emery's place. I spent the day going over a proposal Hudson put together for a luxury condo building in Malibu. We've never owned anything on the coast before, but along with its sweeping ocean views, it boasts a hefty price tag too. Who knows, it may be worth it. Mostly, though, I spent the day glancing at the clock and wondering what Emery was up to while I waited for our non-date to roll around.

When I reach her door, it's already open. "Hello?" I peer inside, not seeing her.

"Come on in," she calls from somewhere inside.

Although one of the smallest models, it's a nice unit, done in neutral colors, and with its tall ceilings and large windows, it feels a lot bigger than it is. I step across the wooden floors, my gaze cutting over to check the kitchen, then the living room with its sleek modern decor. Both are empty.

"Emery?" I call out, wondering what's going on.

"In here. Just finishing up."

I peek around the corner and see her. She's standing in front of the mirror at her bedroom dresser, and though she's facing away from me, I can see her reflection. She's putting on earrings and it's so simple, nothing really, yet I'm transfixed by her.

Dressed casually in jeans and a white tank top, her outfit says this is not a date. But the earrings she's taking the time to put on tell me that she wants me to notice her as a woman, even if she's said she doesn't. This small act signals she's every bit as aware as I am that there's sexual chemistry simmering under the guise of our platonic state. When she turns to face me, her nipples are hardened into two little points, and the dangly gold earrings catch and shimmer in the light. But mostly it's her nipples that I notice because, goddamn, her tits are perfect. A nice, perky mouthful.

"Ready?" she says, her voice soft as she stands there looking at me.

"Yeah." I almost groan as I turn for the door. I'd rather cross the room toward her and toss her down onto her unmade bed. Something tells me we could have a lot of fun between the sheets. Or on the floor. Or in the shower. The image of Emery's creamy skin slippery and wet makes my mouth water.

I use the drive to the restaurant to point out landmarks and celebrity hot spots to Emery. I keep forgetting she's new in town. For some reason, it seems like she's been here a lot longer than a week.

Sunflower Grill is little more than a counter with a chalkboard menu for ordering and a small cluster of tables outside on the sidewalk. Which is good. This isn't a date, and it doesn't feel like one. Being here with Emery actually makes me wonder when the last date I had was. A long damn time ago, apparently, since I can't even remember. We order our food, each paying for ourselves, and then grab a table outside in the shade.

"How was week one on the new job?" I ask once we sit

down. We've both ordered bottles of beer, and I'm glad to see her health kick doesn't preclude her from indulging in alcohol.

"It's actually been really good. I'm working on real cases, drafting briefs, and researching precedents. I get to work directly with the attorneys, and there's a nice girl about my age named Trina who I've been having lunch with."

I nod and take another sip of my beer. "That's awesome. So you like it then?"

She chews on her lower lip. "Yes and no. My boss, Larry The Creeper . . ." She takes a long swig of her beer before continuing. "All week felt like a game of cat and mouse. I tried to avoid him while he doggedly pursued me."

"What do you mean *pursued* you?"

"He wants in my panties," she says matter-of-factly.

I can't stop my lip from curling in disgust. "How old is this guy?"

She shrugs. "Sixty? Give or take."

"Ew."

"Yeah, agreed."

"Did you tell him to fuck off?" I see our server approaching with our food from the corner of my vision.

"No. My hands are tied. It's a long story, but basically that's the fastest way to lose your job. And I can't lose this job."

I growl out a curse. "That's bullshit, but I get what you're saying. Will you let me know if it gets any worse? I'll think of something."

She nods, her gaze tender and locked on mine.

When our food is delivered, I poke at my portabella mushroom cap burger, weary of this experience anew.

"Just try it. It'll be fine," Emery says encouragingly as she digs into her own food.

When I see her take a big, unladylike bite of her black bean quinoa burger and end up with a smear of garlic aioli on her chin, it pretty much makes it worth it coming here. She keeps right on talking about her boss, like nothing even happened. Amused, I lean across the table and use my napkin to wipe her lower lip and chin, smirking at her.

"Did I have something?" She touches her lip.

"I got it."

Now she's the one smirking. "Thanks." After taking another big bite of her sandwich, she reaches over and steals one of my sweet potato fries.

I'm about to tell her to have at 'em, because I won't eat the damn things, when I realize she wasn't waiting for permission. I like that there's no tiptoeing around between us, no *trying to be on our best behavior to impress the other* thing happening. We're just ourselves, and it's comfortable. I'm not sure why I've never had a woman friend before, but I decide this isn't so bad.

"So, Emery," I say, after forcing down another bite of my own meal. "Tell me about this bad breakup you alluded to when we first met." I haven't pried about her past, but now feels like the right time to dive into a deeper conversation. We're full and happy—or least, she is—and we have two fresh beers in front of us, thanks to our server. I lean back in my chair as she fiddles with the label on her bottle.

"Ugh, seriously? You want to know about Asshat McFuckstick?"

I choke on a swig of beer. The poor guy doesn't even deserve a name . . . he must have done something really bad. "Hit me with it."

"Well, the first thing you need to understand is that I'm not coming off of one bad breakup. I'm coming off a trifecta. Three asshole douchebags, each one worse than the last. Apparently I suck at picking guys."

"Lay it on me. It'll be like therapy." I have no idea how to help her, but maybe talking about it will prove to be therapeutic.

She takes a deep swig from her bottle. "I might need something stronger than this."

"Not a problem. My place is fully stocked. We can head back there."

She narrows her eyes. "Nice try, playboy."

Holding up my hands in mock innocence, I smile. "Or we can stay here."

She smiles and leans back in her seat.

"So, what happened with McFuckstick?"

Rolling her eyes, Emery then turns her gaze to the sidewalk and the passing pedestrian traffic. It's a nice evening, and couples and small groups are beginning to venture out to restaurants and bars in the area.

"Well, you're getting ahead of yourself there, Mr. Oliver."

She's still looking away, and I sense she's deflecting the question. Whether it's because she wants to keep the mood lighter, or simply because she's not ready to answer it, I'm not sure, so I wait until she decides to continue.

She sighs. "Before all that mess, first there was Whit and Dana."

I can't help chuckling. "You dated some guys with some pretty feminine names."

Her gaze snaps back to mine, her expression mocking. "Right, because Hayden is the epitome of masculinity."

"Shut it." It's something my own sisters made fun of. I think she's going to elaborate about exes one and two, but instead, her gaze stays out on the street while she takes a long sip of her drink. When Emery leans forward in her chair, gathering up her purse in her lap, I ask, "Are you ready to go?" I figured we'd chill here for a while, so I'm surprised when she seems ready to leave.

She nods. "I'd better. I might try to squeeze in a little more work tonight. Thanks for bringing me here, though, it's a great place."

"Anytime," I say, rising to my feet and helping her from her chair. I'm now regretting my grand idea to pry into her personal life.

As we walk toward the parking garage two blocks away, Emery's quiet and contemplative. I doubt she's thinking about work like she said.

"McFuckstick . . . ," she starts, capturing my attention. "At first it was just the little things, you know? He never wanted to hold my hand because he said it made his hand sweaty." She's quiet when she says this.

I expect her to say something more, but she stares straight ahead with a silent intensity, and I get that this was a big thing to her. A seemingly small thing that reflected on his inability to connect with her, and ended up being a deal-breaker in the end.

Needing to lighten the mood, I decide to humor her. "If I was your boyfriend, I'd hold your hand."

Her gaze cuts over to mine, and a pretty smile adorns her lips. "Well, aren't you sweet. But you'd never be my boyfriend, right?"

"Never ever," I confirm, lacing my fingers between hers.

"Mmm, this feels nice." She gives my hand a squeeze and we continue walking, more in step with each other now that we're linked up.

I find that holding her hand doesn't make mine sweaty at all. It's nice, in fact, and I quickly decide her ex really was a fuckstick.

When we reach my car, I reluctantly let her go, and as she slips into the passenger seat, I immediately miss touching her.

On the ride home, Emery continues her story, and I quickly learn that she has a long list of complaints about her exes. But rightly so. These guys sound like total douches. I'm actually getting a little pissed off as I listen to her talk.

"It was a lot of me, myself, and I back then." She giggles, covering her mouth with her hand. "Oh God, did I just tell you that I used to masturbate a lot?"

"That visual image isn't helping our *friendship*," I say with a sideways glance in her direction. I'm hoping she doesn't notice the erection that's forming in my pants.

"Sorry, but that's the damn truth. Whit couldn't have found the clitoris if I'd drawn him a map."

"That's another thing I can help with." The idea of touching her sweet body makes my cock ache. Even though we're dancing around it, sexual tension burns hotly under the surface, and I can tell from the glances she gives me that she finds me every bit as desirable as I do her.

"Don't be silly," she says, chastising me. "That's what battery-operated boyfriends are for. And they don't cheat or lie."

It pisses me off to know she's had to deal with some unsavory situations. I know she can fend for herself, she's tough and smart and outspoken, but I don't like that she's had that responsibility resting on her shoulders. Men can be scum, and it makes me want to prove to her I'm not just another dipshit from her past.

"What about you?" she asks, suddenly turning the line of questioning on me.

"I definitely know my way around a clit. No worries there. It's all about pressure and speed."

She barks out a laugh. "No, that's not what I meant. Surely you've got a crazy-ex story of your own." She's looking over at me with hopeful eyes, wanting me to take the bait.

Tightening my grip on the steering wheel, I shake my head. "It's not something I want to talk about." We're just starting to get close; I don't want to scare her away yet with the mountain of baggage I'm pulling along behind me.

"Now or ever?" she asks, her tone filled with curiosity.

Ever. But I've just pried into her past, and withholding my own isn't exactly fair. "Now," I settle on.

"Okay." She shrugs. "I'll just have to keep supplying you with vegetarian food and regular yoga classes until I get it out of you."

I grunt. "No way. The next time we go out, I'm choosing what we do. Something manly. Sport fishing, cross-fit, all-you-can-eat Brazilian meats."

She makes a gagging noise next to me, and then laughs. A sweet sound that's full of life and promise, just like her.

When we reach our building, I walk her upstairs, stopping outside her door. She looks beautiful in her simple white cotton tank and jeans; somehow her casual dress makes her look younger than her twenty-four years. I'm filled with desire for her, but I know if she invited me inside right now, I'd fuck everything up.

"Thanks," she murmurs, her wide-set eyes fixed on mine.

Tracing my thumb along her jawline, I revel in how soft her skin is. "Anytime."

Emery's breathing hitches, her only indication that my touch affects her. I want to lean in and kiss her, press my lips to hers, but I won't. Can't.

After a wistful moment, she turns and heads inside, the lock clicking into place once she shuts the door.

"Good night, Emery," I say, and turn to head for my place.

When I get inside, I toss my keys and wallet onto the tray on the counter and sigh. I'm trying to figure out why hanging out with a woman has never felt like that before. It was easy and fun, and I already want to do it again.

Shaking the thoughts away, I open the fridge and peer inside. I'm still fucking starving from that vegetarian dinner. It may work for Emery, but I need meat to sustain me. After making myself a sandwich, I sink down onto the couch and grab the remote. The TV may be playing in the background, but I can't help but recount the cute little things Emery said and did tonight.

Fuck.

Roughly swallowing a bite of roast beef, I sit straight up in my chair. I realize, with stunned horror, that I *like* her. I like hanging out with her. I like her personality, her sass, the fact she has goals. The curve of her hips, her tight ass . . . and the fact that she took the time to put on earrings before our *non-date*.

I'd also like to bang the shit out of her, but I know that isn't possible, both because of my vow to Hudson, and to Beth, but also because it's not what Emery wants or needs. She needs a friend. And that's what I'm going to be.

Setting my unfinished plate aside, I get up and head into the bathroom. I need a cold fucking shower. I need to knock this shit off. I've made a goal for myself, and I'm not going to fuck it up. Even if my dick is rock hard right now just thinking about her.

Quickly stripping down, I step under the spray of lukewarm water. It does nothing to quell my erection, especially since I know that Emery is just one floor below me. She's probably changing into her pajamas, and my mind spins with the possibilities. Does she sleep in a matching shorts-and-tank set, or maybe just her panties and an old T-shirt, her beautiful tits straining against the softened fabric?

My hand finds my cock and I squeeze, trying to quiet the images in my brain. It's no use. The way her round ass filled out those jeans, the hint of cleavage that peeked from her tank top, it's been burned into my brain. Knowing I'm going to give in to temptation, I grab the bottle of body wash, squeeze a generous amount into my palm, and use the suds to stroke my cock up and down. A grunt pushes past my lips as my hand speeds up. My shaft feels like steel and my balls draw up closer to my body.

The images in my brain turn far more salacious . . . Emery naked and kneeling between my feet, her pink lips sucking on the head of my cock, her bent over my bed with her ass up nice and high so I can see her glistening pussy, me pounding into her, showing her what it's like to be fucked by a man who knows what he's doing.

As I pump my fist over the sensitive head of my cock, a strangled moan crawls up my throat and I come hard, sending semen jetting onto the tile below. As the water washes away the evidence of my lack of self-control, I take a deep gulp of air. Jacking off to thoughts of my *friend* isn't normal. I need to lock this shit down. Right the fuck now. But as I towel off, I decide that if this is what I need to do to remain in control around her, so be it.

After my release, I feel a bit more disciplined, my head clearer, and I'm thankful for that. I put on a pair of sweatpants, and then head to the kitchen to grab my phone.

Sitting down on the edge of my bed, I send a text to Emery, inviting her to join me at my nephew's soccer game tomorrow. I figure there's no way I can bend her succulent ass over and fuck her in front of twenty four-year-olds. It's safe, and I need to stick to *safe* activities. Ones where my cock won't get me into trouble.

Because this friends-only thing? It fucking sucks.

Chapter Ten

Emery

I pull into one of the few spots left in the city park's lot. Today has turned out lovely—all sapphire sky, golden sun, and best of all, a low-smog alert—and it seems like all of Los Angeles has come out to enjoy it.

Walking to the soccer field, I look around until I see Hayden waving from the bleachers. There's a cute couple with him that must be his sister and her husband. *What are their names again?* I try to remember. Hayden mentioned them in his text. *Beth and . . . Daniel? No, David.*

Beth is sitting on the bottom row of steps with a princess no older than three conked out on her lap. It's amazing what little kids can sleep through; despite all the children shrieking and adults laughing around her, this girl is out cold. I can see the family resemblance to both her mother and to Hayden—the same dark hair, the same high forehead, the same straight nose.

A slightly older boy clings to David, his free hand gripping a box of apple juice. His messy nut-brown hair makes him look more like his father. He looks up at me with huge blue-gray eyes. When I smile and wave back at him, he grins and hides his face in his father's pant leg.

David chuckles and pats his son on the head. "He likes you."

"Careful, Hayden," Beth says with a smirk. "You've got competition." She reaches out and takes my hand, giving it a warm shake.

Hayden's eyes swing over to mine, and a warm shiver runs along my body. "You came."

I nod. "Of course I did. It's beautiful out today."

He and Beth both look up at the sky, trying to figure out what I mean. It's LA—every day is pretty much the same. I guess this Midwest girl isn't used to that yet.

Noticing that his nephew is still hiding his face in David's leg, Hayden squats down to the boy's level. "Hey there, Austin. How's my buddy? I invited my friend Emery to watch you play today." The boy grunts and buries his face even more. "You want a high-five?" Hayden says, holding up his hand.

Giggling, Austin bats at it with his juice box, squirting sticky sugar water all over his uncle's hand.

Hayden's air of cheerful calm doesn't diminish. "You excited to play today?"

Austin finally speaks up. "Yeah. I'm gonna soccer."

"He cried on the way here," Beth interjects. "He wanted to wear his dinosaur shirt, but we put him in his league uniform, so . . . you can guess."

A stout man in a baseball cap walks onto the turf and blows his whistle. The chaos of parents and kids all around us spikes to a crescendo.

"Looks like it's time to get on the field." David bends down to take Austin's hand. "Ready to go see your friends?"

"No," Austin says.

"Come on, little dude. Don't you want to—"

Austin screams so loudly and so suddenly that I jump. His sister squirms in Beth's arms, still half-asleep.

David sighs. "Hayden, can you take him somewhere quiet? I have to get his bag from the car."

"No problem." Hayden scoops up the flailing Austin and walks off toward a nearby stand of trees.

When both men have left, Beth turns to me. "Sorry about that," she says, stroking her daughter's raven hair to soothe her. "I think he's just overstimulated. He loves soccer, but sometimes all the people and noise and activity . . ." She makes a *bzzt* noise. "Blows a fuse."

I shake my head with a smile. "Don't worry about it. Life is tough when you're a kid."

"Heh . . . tell me about it. Hayden's great with him, though. Which is a huge help. David and I didn't get much sleep last night. Georgia kept waking up all night with some weird dream. Too much candy before bed." Beth dips her head to indicate her daughter, who is already comatose on her lap again. Then she hesitates. "When Hayden mentioned he'd be bringing a girl . . . I gotta say, I didn't expect you."

Now she has my attention. Any chance I can get to dig up some dirt on Hayden, I'm game. Especially because I want a point of reference that isn't Roxy's. I sit down next to Beth on the bleachers. "What do you mean?"

"Hayden doesn't usually hang around . . . you know. The kind of women you bring to meet your family."

Two uncomfortable ideas hit me at once. One of them is: *Meeting his family? Is that what this is all about? Am I being evaluated?* And the other: *Was Roxy right after all?* Hayden doesn't date girls long enough to introduce them to anyone. He doesn't bother with "nice girls" at all; he aims for the women he can pump and dump. So how long is he going to bother with me, in my frumpy T-shirt and worn tennis shoes and a streak of white sunscreen on my nose?

Beth's casual comment has unleashed fears I didn't even know I had. I make a mental note to mend fences with Roxy; she was only trying to look out for me after all.

I'm suddenly aware that I've been silent for too long. I lick my dry lips nervously, trying to figure out how to respond to Beth. "Well," I finally say, "I mean, we're just friends. I'm not . . ." *Not interested, I swear.* "I don't need to be his type."

"Oh," Beth says, drawing out the sound into a long note of realization. "I'm sorry. I just assumed you were his date."

Do I want to be his date? Am I that lonely and horny? What am I even doing here?

Beth interrupts my torrent of thoughts by pointing at the field. "Looks like things are under control now."

There are almost two dozen little kids scattered over the turf, dressed in either red or blue. Evidently toddler soccer is more popular around here than I would have guessed. I note with relief that Austin is among them.

David and Hayden come back to the bleachers and we settle in to watch the game. But as much as I try to concentrate, I'm too aware of Hayden's warm, solid body pressed up against my shoulder and thigh. And Beth's comments about him never bringing nice normal girls around buzz through my head.

• • •

The game ends in a one-to-one tie. The players did more shouting, giggling, and rolling on the grass than actual soccer, and the referee called several time-outs for temper tantrums or crying over scraped knees. But the kids seem like they had a good time, which is the whole point of sports anyway. And watching them run around in circles chasing the ball was adorable.

As soon as David suggests going to a local pizzeria to celebrate, Georgia snaps awake. She insistently repeats *peese-a, peese-a* all the way across the parking lot until we separate into our own cars. And now I'm sitting with Hayden's extended family again, crammed into a plastic booth in a loud, colorful restaurant.

His younger sister, Gracie, who's closer to my age, arrives and slips into the booth next to Hayden. Her eyes land on me, and when Beth introduces me as Hayden's new *friend*, Gracie's eyes go as wide as the plates on our table.

"Oh. Um . . . hi?" she says, offering me her hand across the table.

It's like I'm the main attraction at a freak show. I take

her hand and shake it. "Hello."

I have no idea what to say next. Gracie is gorgeous. Where Beth is put together in a no-nonsense way, with her bobbed haircut and friendly eyes, Gracie exudes an air of feminine beauty and innocence. Wide-set blue eyes and tousled wavy hair that's chestnut-colored, but with flecks of gold where it catches the light. Her high cheekbones and pouty lips make me envious. Having nothing else to say, I glance back over to Hayden.

I'm watching him bounce his tiny niece on his knee and feed her bites of cheesy bread. And I'm still wondering what the hell I'm doing here. What this all means; what I should do next.

I'm confused all over again, and I have no idea how to feel. Hayden is so sweet with his nephew and niece, so playfully combative with his sisters, so chummy with his brother-in-law—he's clearly capable of love and affection. So why is he so closed off when it comes to women?

He still hasn't opened up about his past, no matter how much I prod and poke. Did something specific sour him on romantic relationships? Is he distrustful because he's scared? What happened to make him this way?

I want to corner Beth and ask her, but something tells me she may be more forthcoming with information if I can get her away from all these distractions—and pump her full of sangria. I make a mental note.

Georgia is an absolute mess, with sauce smeared all over her face and the front of her frilly dress. Hayden is laughing and tickling her. Beth and David are fussing over Austin. Gracie sits quietly, taking it all in with a fond smile.

Watching them, despite my confusion, I can't help but feel content. Strangely soothed. They're a picture-perfect family. And Hayden's grin—unrestrained, dimples showing, blue eyes crinkled almost shut as he laughs—is nothing short of beautiful.

I remember the way he touched my face after dinner on Saturday. I felt an unmistakable spark of warmth and wanted to lean into his hand, wanted him to . . .

But none of that should ever happen. It's best that nothing *did* happen that night. Even if we both feel funny in our pants for each other, sex just isn't a good idea. We won't work in the long run. Period.

So then . . . what *do* we do? Continue this friendship that nobody seems to think Hayden is capable of? In the end I just eat my mushroom pizza, drink my soda, and let myself soak in the warm, comfortable atmosphere. And if I admire Hayden more than I should, I don't think too hard about it. Because there's nothing to think about.

Hayden and I arrive back home at the same time. We walk together through the front entrance and upstairs to my door. "Thanks for coming," he says as I unlock it. "It was nice to have another grown-up in the mix."

I turn to him, my keys still dangling from the lock. I want to ask why he invited me today. I want to ask why he ever started talking to me in the first place. But all I say is, "Sure . . . thanks for inviting me. I had fun."

He opens his arms slightly. "Hug good-bye?" His crooked smile says that if I don't accept, he'll pass it off as a joke. Something he never really meant in the first place.

I hesitate for a second, then step into his embrace. He is so warm, so solid and real, and it's been such a long time since I've been touched. I inhale his cologne, that same smoky spice that riveted me the first moment we met. My cheek rests against his neck where smoothness meets stubble, and I can feel his pulse fluttering. I can feel the angled, muscular body under his casual clothes. And one very particular angle pressing into my stomach . . .

I pull back my head just far enough to look into his stunning eyes. "Stunning" is exactly the right word— they paralyze me, pin me, make me helpless. Our mouths are less than an inch apart, and I realize that my heart is hammering. Just as fast as his.

Desire and fear make me brave . . . or maybe just stupid. "What are we doing?" I ask him, not meaning for it to sound like a plea.

"Being friends," he replies. His breath puffs over my lips, and I almost shiver. "Why do you ask?"

"Because friends don't usually get erections for each other, do they?" I retort without any real force, bumping my hip into the large ridge in his shorts. *Friends also don't get soaking-wet panties, for that matter.*

Hayden glances down and away, looking something close to frustrated. "I just . . . haven't gotten any action in a while. Ignore me. It doesn't mean anything."

He's probably just saying that to defuse an awkward situation. But it still kind of stings to hear "it doesn't mean anything" about a boner that I assumed was for me. *I hoped was for me.*

I nod, stepping away long after I should have. "If you say so."

"You want to do something next Saturday? Maybe get dinner again?" he asks casually, as if everything were totally normal and not a big confusing horny mess. Fuck, I mean these panties are literally destroyed. From one hug.

"Um . . . sure." *Why the hell not.* For no real reason, I nod again. "I'll text you tomorrow."

He smiles and raises his hand in a half wave. "Good night, Emery."

I watch him walk down the hall and disappear up the stairs, and then I finally go inside. As I get ready for bed, my mind keeps spinning on and on about Hayden. I replay and dissect every word I've heard today while I shower, brush my teeth, and change into pajamas.

He said he hasn't gotten any action lately. But why not? Why isn't he sleeping around like he usually does? Maybe he just said that to brush me off. But it suddenly occurs to me that he never seems to be unavailable. Whenever I text him, he always replies within an hour, and he's free practically anytime I want to hang out. Is he spending all his spare moments with me? Is that why he isn't getting laid?

I don't know what this means. I don't even know how I feel about it. I bury my face in the pillow, ready to give up and go to sleep.

Just as I start to drift off, my phone rings. Groaning, I roll over and grab it. "Hello?"

"Hi, sweet pea," Mom cries out, her voice cheerfully loud. I can hear rumbling engines and crunching gravel in the background; she must be at the truck depot.

"How are you?"

I prop myself up on my elbow and squint at the alarm clock. "Uh . . . I'm fine. What's up?"

"I know this is short notice, and I'm sure you're busy with work, but I got a last-minute delivery to Pasadena. Some kind of electronics parts, I don't have the manifest in front of me. Anyway, I'll be in your neck of the woods on Saturday, so I'd love to get lunch if you have time."

"That sounds great, Mom. I'll take a half day on Saturday and come out to see you."

"Oh, how wonderful." I can practically see her beaming. "You have to tell me everything you've been up to. I'm so proud of my smart girl."

As soon as I arrange to meet her at a Pasadena diner and hang up, I remember that I told Hayden we'd hang out next weekend. "Shit," I grumble aloud. I grab my phone again and tap out a quick text.

*EMERY: Can we do Sunday instead of Saturday? My
      mom's coming and she's only in town for a couple days.*

Two minutes later, my phone chimes with a reply.

*HAYDEN: That's cool. Let me know if you need any ideas
      for what to do while she's in town.*

EMERY: Hmm. Not sure. She'll be in Pasadena.

*HAYDEN: I can give you a ride. I should visit Pasadena
      anyway and meet the building manager about rent . . .
      Caltech grad students are poor as fuck.*

I pause to consider his offer, my thumb hovering over
the keypad. On the one hand, I don't want anything to
interrupt my time with Mom. It would suck if we had to
cut our lunch short because Hayden needed to get back
to Los Angeles. On the other, I could avoid dealing with
the utter hell that is southern California traffic. Let
Hayden raise his blood pressure for me.

As I'm thinking, I get another text.

HAYDEN: It'd be fun to meet your mom, she must be amazing lady if she made you. ;) You saw my awkward family today, I should get to see yours.

That's an unexpectedly good point. It still feels a little weird for us to be meeting each other's relatives all of a sudden, but if I introduce Mom and Hayden, maybe I could ask her for a second opinion. Or maybe it's a fourth opinion by this point, after all the people who've warned me about him.

Before I can change my mind, I send a reply.

EMERY: I guess that's only fair. Pick me up at work on Saturday at 11 AM?

I wait for his confirmation—a simple *OK*—before I turn off my phone and finally sleep.

• • •

When we walk into the diner on Saturday, Mom is already sitting in a booth with a huge hamburger in front of her. "Over here," she calls with a wave. "I'm starved, so I went ahead and ordered."

Hayden looks slightly startled. He probably expected this little old lady with thick bifocals and thinning gray hair—but the plaid flannel shirt and the hat proudly emblazoned with MOTHER TRUCKER in tall red letters, not so much. To his credit, he only pauses for a moment before replying, "We don't mind. I'm only staying for a cup of coffee anyway."

We sit down facing her. Hayden orders his coffee and I get blueberry pancakes. Breakfast is just about the only meat-free thing on the menu here.

After the waitress leaves, I reach out to hold Mom's hands. My heart twists a little; her wrists and knuckles seem even stiffer than when I left home. "You've got to stop running these long hauls, Mom. The doctor said that manual transmission is wrecking your joints. And what if you get a blood clot in your legs from sitting eleven hours a day?"

"Nonsense," she huffs. "Best job I ever had. Fifty-five grand a year, I decide my own schedule, and I get to see the country. You think waiting tables again would be easier on my knees? And my hands and shoulders are too shot to go back to factory jobs."

"But you don't need to work so hard anymore. You can stick to local deliveries. I'm done with school, and I'm making my own loan payments and living off my own savings. In a few years, I'll start earning enough that you can retire."

"I'm not here to talk about me, sweet pea. Or about money. I want to hear what's new with you." She cocks her head with a sly smile. "And who's your friend?"

"I'm Hayden," he says, standing up awkwardly in the booth and extending his hand. "Nice to meet you, Mrs. Winters."

Mom shakes his hand and he blinks; another thing he clearly didn't expect is her patented death grip. "Call me Val. You work at Emery's firm?"

For the next twenty minutes, Mom peppers Hayden

with questions about how we met, what he does for a living, where he went to school. He answers everything with as much grace as an interrogated prisoner can muster.

I give up even trying to steer the conversation. Mom has always thrown herself full force into everything—she's known for her fierce affection, fierce anger, fierce joy— and it's impossible to stop her once she's made a decision.

Eventually Hayden finishes his coffee, leaves a fifty-dollar bill on the table to cover all three of our checks, and gets the hell out of there before I can protest his generosity. As soon as the door clangs shut behind him, Mom fixes me with a keen stare over her wire frames. "Don't fall in love with that boy."

I splutter out my mouthful of iced tea. "W-what?"

"You heard me," Mom says calmly. "I'm crazy, not stupid. I see the way you look at him. I understand . . . he's handsome as all get-out, and he seems pretty smart too. But he isn't the type to settle down. Don't put stock into what'll never be."

A strange heaviness settles in the pit of my stomach. When I came here, I thought that Mom's advice would quiet my restless thoughts and give me direction. Then why don't I feel any better? Actually, I might even feel worse. I busy myself wiping up my spilled tea, chewing the inside of my lip.

"I know what he's like, Mom," I finally say. "Don't worry . . . we're just friends."

She nods a few times. "Good girl. I didn't raise no fool."

"No, Mom. You sure didn't," I say to reassure her, wondering if I'm lying.

Chapter Eleven

Hayden

"What the hell are these?" Dottie's shrill voice calls as she comes out of my bedroom with a purple G-string dangling from her little finger.

I shrug. "No idea."

Her face twists in disgust. "They were under your bed. What do you mean you have no idea?"

Her tone is accusatory, but I really have no clue. I haven't had a woman here in weeks, and just with that thought alone, my cock aches in a silent plea for relief. I realize I haven't gotten any since Emery moved in. That strikes me as odd, and I have no explanation for it. Realizing that Dottie is still talking to me, I blink away the thoughts.

She gives me a reproving look. "Nice girls don't wear the kind of panties I find in your bed. Crotchless G-strings are for strippers and bad girls. I want you to settle down with a good girl, Hayden," she says, tossing the panties into the garbage like they're diseased.

"I know you do, Dottie, and I appreciate that."

Dottie comes three times a week to clean up, do laundry, cook, pick up my dry cleaning, and run errands. She's sixty, but with more energy than the Energizer Bunny. She keeps my life running smoothly. I don't want to do anything to piss her off, so I usually nod and smile at whatever piece of wisdom she's offering up. But today, I'm stuck trying to figure out who those undies can possibly belong to.

I cross the room to where Dottie is wiping down the countertop. "I've got to run. Don't stay too late." I press a kiss to her cheek. She's like a second mother to me, and even if I do write her paycheck, her concern and care for me always feel genuine.

She shoos me away. "I'll stay until I'm happy that everything's done. Have fun."

I nod, grabbing my keys. I'm meeting Hudson for some beers. It's been too long since we've hung out just as friends, without the worry of work hanging between us.

I head to The Avenue, a bar that's become a regular meet-up spot for us. It's on the edge of downtown about halfway between where he and I live, and it has an upscale feel without being swanky. The drinks are always cold, and the food is good too. When I pull into the parking lot, I spot his luxury SUV right away. Strolling inside, I find the coolness of the air-conditioning is welcome against my skin.

He's sitting at the bar with a bottle of beer already in his hand and another waiting for me in front of the stool next to him. God bless America.

"Hey, buddy, how've you been?" I say, sliding onto the bar stool next to him.

He raises his bottle and clinks it to mine. "Life's been pretty damn good lately. I haven't had any angry tenants to deal with."

I smirk at him. "I'm following through. You didn't doubt me, did you?"

His eyebrows jump up. "Fuck yeah, I did. Especially when you started hanging out with the hot-as-fuck new girl."

"Emery," I remind him. "And we're still hanging out."

"No shit? As friends, huh?"

I nod, taking a sip of my beer and feeling oddly proud. "We've been out to eat, and worked out a couple times together." He doesn't need to know it was yoga. That would just be weird.

"I'm impressed, dude. I didn't think you had it in you."

"Yup. Strictly platonic."

Except last weekend when I hugged her good-bye and got a huge erection that was impossible to hide. Emery even called me out—asking me to explain myself. I lied and said it was nothing, and I swear the flash of disappointment across her face almost killed me. I wanted to tell her right then and there how insanely attracted to her I was, how beautiful she looked that day in her casual clothes, hanging out with my family.

"So where have you been getting your good time?" Hudson looks genuinely confused.

"I'm on a bit of a dry spell," I admit. "You've thrown

off my game." I jab him in the ribs before taking another swig of my beer to try to forget all about that encounter with Emery.

He shakes his head at me. "Don't blame this on me. Maybe you have real feelings for this one. That could be a good thing. Get you back up on the horse, so to speak."

"No, it's not like that between us. Emery's sworn off men, and you know I'm sure as shit not looking for a relationship."

"Yes, but I'm saying maybe it's time to move on. Grow up a little." His gaze abandons the TV and swings over to mine. "Have you ever been really into a chick? You know, the big L-word?"

"Are you trying to ask me if I've ever been in love with a woman before?"

He nods. "Yeah, I guess so."

"Sure," I say.

Hudson levels me with that dark, intense stare of his.

"What?" My tone is both playful and defensive. This really isn't something I want to discuss. I'd rather be talking about work, anything other than the state of my love life.

"I'm not buying it, Oliver. You're so damn closed off from anything real, it's not even funny. After Naomi—"

I shut him up with a wave of my hand. "Forget Naomi. I was close to a girl once. She let out a loud, thunderous fart in her sleep, and that was it. I ended things after that."

"You broke up with a girl for farting?"

"Indeed," I confirm.

"That wasn't love, then."

"How do you know? Kelsey . . . or was it Kerrie? Anyway, she was sweet and funny, and she made a hell of a ham sandwich."

Hudson shakes his head. "Because when you're in love, and your woman feels comfortable enough to do that in front of you, you'll think it's cute."

"I'll think farting is cute? Not a chance in hell." Women

don't shit, or fart, or belch as far as I'm concerned. And Hudson's lost his damn mind.

"Trust me on this one."

I don't trust him any farther than I can throw him—and considering he clears six foot two and is solid muscle, it wouldn't be very damn far.

"You been seeing anyone interesting lately?" I ask.

Hudson doesn't sleep around with our tenants, like I used to enjoy before he abruptly put a stop to that, but he definitely gets his fair share of pussy. Not that I'm overly interested; I'm just eager to steer the conversation to his love life and away from mine.

"How's your sister?" he asks out of the blue.

"Beth's doing the supermom thing. Same old."

"No, I meant Gracie." His eyes dart away from mine, as if there's something he doesn't want me to see. I try not to read too much into it. Hudson would never betray me by going after my sister. Plus, he's too busy fucking his way through the female population, one leggy blonde at a time. Which Gracie is most definitely not.

I shrug. "Gracie's Gracie." She's always been my innocent little sister. It's crazy to think she's twenty-two now and just graduated from college.

Hudson nods once, effectively ending that weird conversation. *Okay then.*

Chapter Twelve

Emery

As the weeks pass and my bar exam looms closer, I
ramp up my studying. But I still find spare hours here
and there to spend with Hayden. He fully lives up to his
promise to show me around the city. We explore not
only the typical tourist stuff, like the Walk of Fame and
the La Brea tar pits, but all the hidden gems that he's
learned about from his years in Los Angeles. My earlier
anxieties soon melt away, leaving me upbeat when I'm
around him and optimistic when I'm away. Everything
has turned out fine; this friendship is totally working.
I'm glad I didn't listen to Roxy after all.

Early one Wednesday, when all the law staff file into the
conference room for our weekly meeting, Mr. Pratt is
already standing at the head of the table. He starts
strolling around like he's King Arthur surveying his
knights. "I want to thank you for all your hard work
these past two months. We met not only a tough
deadline, but the high standards of quality that Walker,

Price, and Pratt is known for. We have a reputation among the best corporate law firms, and I can honestly say that you've lived up to it . . ."

He blathers on for a few more minutes in that vein. Even though his speech is more than a little corny, pride surges warm in my chest, knowing I played a role in helping. This merger was my first real case. *I'm actually doing law,* I think with a thrum of excitement. *I'm practically a bona fide lawyer already. Booyah.*

Mr. Pratt pauses beside my seat. "In fact, our client is so pleased with our work, they've invited us to their annual company get-together in Omaha. We fly in next Monday afternoon, stay at the luxury hotel they've booked, and fly back first thing on Thursday morning." He speaks over the burst of muttering among the other lawyers in the room. "There's a few loose ends to tie up—some business is best done in person, as I'm sure you all know. But primarily, we're celebrating a job well done. All expenses paid. You can even bring a guest."

He plunks his hand down next to mine, looming over me and brushing his arm against my shoulder. He's close enough for me to smell tuna when he exhales, and my gag reflex kicks in like a motherfucker. I just barely keep down my latte.

Everything about this moment is so disturbing. It's not even ten in the morning—why the hell does he have fish breath? I wonder if I can get away with "accidentally" rolling my chair over his foot. Even if he doesn't back off, I'd love to see those spit-polished wingtips scuffed.

"And since you've been such a valuable pinch hitter, Emery, that invitation includes you." He winks at me with a crooked smirk. *Oh, barf.* "I look forward to spending some time together outside the office. Getting to know each other in a more intimate setting."

My stomach yanks itself inside out. Three nights alone in a hotel with Larry The Creeper? In a strange city over a thousand miles from anywhere I know, anywhere I can easily bail out to? *Fuck that noise* doesn't even begin to cover it. There isn't a swear word in the English language strong enough to capture the sheer depths of my "nope."

"Um . . ." It's hard to think over the screaming of my

fight-or-flight instincts. Life would be so much easier if I could just knee him in the balls and run out of the room. "You know, I wish I could, but I don't think I can go. I need to study for the bar, and there's the other cases we've put off while working on this merger . . ."

He shakes his head. "I'm afraid it'll look bad if you don't come. You're a member of our team, after all. And I've already RSVP'd for eight people."

Somehow I think he's more concerned about his boner's feelings than the client's. The client probably doesn't even know I exist. But I can't argue with my boss about how they would hypothetically react. He would just insist that he knows them better than I do, which is true. Whatever excuse I come up with, he'll just shoot it down—or skip straight to pulling rank on me. He's clearly hell-bent on trapping me in an Omaha hotel with him.

I don't think he'd go so far as to *try* anything, but you never know with a dirty old man like that. And even in the best-case scenario, I'd have to put up with his disgusting come-ons and wandering hands for three nights straight. I might jump off the damn hotel roof.

Think, Emery, think. My eyes dart wildly around the room. The other lawyers are muttering about the arrangements for this impromptu "vacation," and I hear a couple of them mention bringing their wives. That's it—I just need a buffer. Someone to keep Mr. Pratt from thinking that we'll spend even a single minute alone together.

"In that case, I guess I can spare the time." I look up to give Mr. Pratt a plastic smile. "My boyfriend will be so excited. He's a big Mavericks fan." I give Mom a silent thank-you for her obsession with college football; all the sports trivia I absorbed in childhood has helped me bullshit annoying men before, and this won't be the last time.

"Your boyfriend?" It's unbelievably satisfying to watch Mr. Pratt's face fall and crash into a million pieces. "Ah . . . yes, of course he's welcome."

I mentally pump my fist. After telling us that we can bring guests, even the master lawyer can't talk his way back out of this one.

But I can't savor my victory for long. Now I have to

figure out how to talk Hayden into flying halfway across America to sit around with stuffy corporate types in an endless cornfield. We've started to become pretty good friends by now, but abandoning his responsibilities for half a week to play bodyguard is a huge favor.

And will this make things weird between us? Will Hayden think I'm asking for more than just a travel buddy? Even if we aren't expected to share a room, God forbid, we'll still be isolated in kind of an intimate way. The mere situation may put ideas into his head.

Hell, the party atmosphere and unlimited free drinks may go to *my* head. I've accepted that our sexual tension is both here to stay and best left unresolved. I don't want to do anything stupid to upset the status quo. Yet there's no denying that the lack of orgasms is really starting to piss me off. I need things stuck in places, things licked and sucked that aren't polite to mention in mixed company.

The staff meeting breaks up as everyone heads back to their desks or downstairs for lunch. I grab my brown paper sack—falafel pita with hummus and Bermuda onion today, *yum, yum*—and make a beeline for the reception desk. Eating with Trina will help preserve my sanity.

The first thing she says to me once we sit down for lunch is, "You look like someone just kidnapped your dog."

"I don't have time for this elbow-rubbing crap," I moan between bites. "The bar exam is in less than three weeks. I need to focus on studying. But does anybody give a damn?"

"I feel your pain, babe." Trina sips her lemonade. Her fingernails are painted forest green this week. "My certification is also coming up fast. Like the label on car mirrors . . . PANIC MAY BE CLOSER THAN IT APPEARS."

"What's your anti-Larry strategy for this trip?" I ask. My joking tone rings a little hollow, even to my own ears. "Bestow your hallowed secrets upon me, mighty Pervert Whisperer."

She shrugs with a smile that's half amused and half pitying. "I wasn't invited, so I don't have to deal with him at all. The perks of being a lowly paper monkey."

I chew and swallow an extra-smelly bite of my pita. My breath is going to be horrendous after this. *Perfect.* "You know, I still don't get it. You should be a rising star at some firm by now. I don't understand why you're a legal secretary in the first place, and paralegal seems like kind of a low bar to aim for. You're smarter and more diligent than half the associates here."

Trina snorts, not unkindly. "What, you think people only take assistant-type jobs because they're too stupid for law school? I've spent two years watching everyone at this firm run around like chickens with their heads cut off. No thanks, I'll pass."

"So you don't like law? Then why work in the field at all?"

"I didn't say that. I think law is interesting. But it's just my living, not my life, you know? Maybe I could hack it as a lawyer. If I did, I'd sure make more money. But the ulcers and marathon hours aren't worth it to me. Walker and Price probably see me more often than they see their own wives, and I think that's fucking sad."

I ponder as I slowly chew my latest mouthful. *So . . . which is it? Does she like law or not?* I can't quite wrap my head around what she's saying. If law interests her, then why not go whole hog? And if she doesn't want to go whole hog, then why bother at all? Why work in a career that doesn't fully capture your heart? Either you love something or you can live without it.

Mistaking my furrowed brow for hurt feelings, Trina hurries to add, "I mean . . . if you want the prestige, or the money, or you just love sweating over contracts from dawn 'til dusk, more power to you. But I guess I'm just not an ambitious type. I'm not interested in climbing any corporate ladders. All I care about is having enough money to do what I want in the other fifteen hours of the day." She pauses to glance around in case Mr. Pratt is lurking nearby. "And finding another job with a normal boss. So I'm making myself more marketable."

I make a thoughtful noise; even if my mouth weren't full of falafel, I wouldn't be sure how to respond. I guess I can see where she's coming from. She's satisfied with her life as it stands now, so she goes with its flow. It's still hard to imagine life from her perspective, though. I have so much to do before I reach that point of contented stability: pass the bar exam, officially join a firm, get promoted until I earn enough for both Mom and myself.

And even then, I don't think anything could ever come before my career. I'm the opposite of Trina—law is my life, not just my living. It's part of who I am. You could bury me in work and I'd beg for more. Sick, I know.

Neither of us is right or wrong; we're just different people with different priorities. Still, that tiny insight into Trina's mind makes me think. She was talking about work, not relationships, but maybe I can apply a little of her attitude toward my situation with Hayden. *Heh . . . talk about people who take life one step at a time.*

Maybe I don't need a master plan for every single thing. Maybe it's okay to play our friendship by ear and stop sweating the small stuff. I want Hayden's help, so I'll ask him for it. Boom. Simple as that. The worst that can happen is he says no and I have to figure out another solution to deal with Mr. Grabby Hands on my own.

But it will probably still help if I butter him up first. I should at least pay a visit to his place—asking favors usually goes over better in person. Especially if I bring some good beer. And there's no possibility of him ignoring me and pretending he just didn't see my text.

• • •

That night after work, I knock on Hayden's door with a six-pack of chilled microbrew. He lets me in, making a comment about how I'm turning out to be the perfect friend, bringing cold beer to his place and all.

I wander inside, glancing around with curiosity while he puts the beer in the fridge. Hayden's condo looks like a typical rich-boy bachelor pad with lots of sleek gadgets, black leather furniture, and pop-art prints on the walls. But it's cleaner and neater than I expected.

When an older lady bustles out of his bedroom carrying a basket heaping with dirty laundry, I realize why the place looks so nice. This flower-aproned woman must be Hayden's housekeeper. She looks around Mom's age and she's just as energetic, but that's where the similarities end. Where my mother is short and stout—"built like a brick shithouse," as she would put it—the housekeeper is almost as wispy as her cloud of dyed black hair.

Hayden turns to follow my gaze. "Oh my God, Dottie, don't lift that heavy crap. I can wash my own clothes when I'm home."

"But you have a guest," she protests. Her voice is strident and reedy, with what may be a faint Southern twang—another point of contrast to Mom's low, drawling tones. "You can't run 'round with chores and leave your lady friend to sit. It's rude."

I try to say that I don't mind, but neither of them pay any attention.

"Then I'll do laundry after she leaves," Hayden replies. "Why don't you take a break and put your feet up? You've been here working all day." He points to the kitchen. "You want to have a beer with us?"

"Well, if you insist . . . just for a moment. And water is fine." She sets his laundry down by the living room doorway and perches on the edge of the armchair like a restless bird.

My lips quirk; it's endearing to see Hayden fuss over her, as if she were family instead of his employee.

He retrieves a bottle of water and two beers from the

fridge and I focus again on the reason why I came here. Despite my determination, I feel a little squirm of nervousness. He probably isn't going to like my Omaha plan, and there's only so much I can say to persuade him before things devolve into begging and awkward silence.

As Hayden hands me my opened beer, I pluck up my courage and say brightly, "Hey, can I ask you a favor?"

He gives me a weird look. "That depends on what it is."

Shit, he's already suspicious. I guess I knew he wasn't stupid. And I'm probably not the first woman to try to sweet-talk him into trouble. *Nothing to do now but dive right in.*

"I have a work thing in Omaha next week," I start. "We'll be staying at a hotel for two nights, and I'm sure my gross boss is going to pester me for the entire trip." I take a deep breath. "Will you come with me as my shield? Just so I don't have to be alone with him?"

His brow is furrowed. "Omaha. As in, Nebraska."

"Pretty please? You're the only friend I can ask. If I

brought a woman, he'd just perv all over her too."
Hopefully Hayden's loyalty to me wins out over his
desire to stay out of this mess. "Come on . . . it's
basically one giant party. All the free steak and whiskey
you can handle."

"I don't know," he says with mock thoughtfulness. "I
can handle a lot when it comes to meat and liquor."

"Well, that'll be their problem, won't it? They promised
unlimited refreshments." I smile sweetly.

"Oh, come on," Dottie chimes in. I wasn't even aware
she was listening. "A beautiful girl invites you on
vacation, what's there to think about?"

While it's not exactly a vacation, and I'm definitely not
one of Hayden's latest conquests looking for some fun
between the sheets, Dottie's enthusiasm is cute. *Lies. All
lies.* I would bounce on that pogo stick for hours.

Hayden rubs his chin, then takes out his phone. "Let me
check my calendar. I might have to move some
appointments around. When does the flight leave?"

I give him all the travel details, sternly telling myself not
to get my hopes up, and sit on the couch to wait while

he taps at his phone. Dottie has gotten to her feet again, and I politely turn down her insistent offers to fix me something to eat.

Eventually Hayden puts down the phone and gives me a reassuring smile. "There . . . all taken care of. I'll come with you."

"You're a lifesaver," I say on a relieved breath, really meaning it. "Thank you so much."

"Hey, no problem. I'm happy to help out a friend." He chuckles. "The free food and booze is just a bonus."

Smiling back at Hayden, I can feel my whole body relax. Of course he would come through for me. Why was I freaking out about this earlier? I never should have worried about where our friendship stands or where it might go. Whatever it is we have, it doesn't have to be anything in particular. It can just *exist*—in whatever way feels right.

"You have plans for dinner?" he asks, capturing my attention again with his sweet charm and megawatt smile.

God, the things this man does to me without having any awareness. I'm surprised I haven't melted into a horny, needy puddle yet.

"No, but I need to crank through some serious studying tonight. I'll probably just order a pizza or something."

He smirks at me. "I've seen the Gio's delivery driver here three times this week. Aren't you sick of pizza yet?"

Rolling my eyes, I take another sip of my beer. "What are you, the carbohydrate police? Can't a girl enjoy a veggie pizza three times a week?"

"Listen." He stands, rising to his full height above me. "I'm going to cook. You've gotta eat. It's a no-brainer. Go get your books or whatever, and I'll start whipping us up something."

"You cook?"

He shrugs. "On occasion."

Knowing that it would be in poor taste to argue with him just when he's cleared his calendar and agreed to come to Omaha with me, I comply, scurrying down the stairs to grab my laptop and notebook. I doubt I'll get much studying done, but he's right about me needing to eat.

When I come back, three distinct things have changed. One—Dottie has left for the day. Two—there's soft jazz music playing in the background. Three—Hayden's tight ass looks damn good in the pair of dark jeans he's wearing. Well, maybe that hasn't changed, I just can fully appreciate it since he's stationed himself at the kitchen island. He's just finishing a phone call, complete with an *I love you* at the end.

Curiosity tempting me, I wander into the kitchen. "Who was that?" I ask.

"My little sister Gracie. She wanted to tell me she got the job she interviewed for."

"Oh, that's great."

His sisters were both so nice and pretty, and it's cool how he's close with them. You can't be that bad of a guy and be super tight with your sisters, right? I picture myself shopping with them, having pedicure dates and sharing bottles of wine . . .

I stomp down that line of thinking as quickly as I can. Hayden and I aren't together, so why am I planning all of this about a guy who's supposed to be my friend?

"What are you making?" I ask, peering around his shoulder. I'm expecting little more than boxed macaroni and cheese, or maybe a can of soup, and am pleasantly surprised to see him cleaning baby cremini mushrooms.

"Mushroom risotto. And a salad on the side."

"Hmm." I don't know quite what else to say. Did he really just have all the ingredients for a vegetarian dinner just lying around, or did he plan this?

"Wash that cucumber for me, would you?" He tilts his chin to the sink, where a colander waits with a large vibrant green cucumber inside.

"Sure." I head over to the sink and begin by washing my hands, then rinse off the cucumber. Lost in my thoughts about how in the world I'm going to find time for all the studying that still needs to happen between now and the bar exam, I'm surprised when the sound of Hayden clearing his throat interrupts me.

He's watching me intently, his eyes burning with something hot and intense. I look down at my hands and realize my movements have been a little lewd.

"I hope I'm next." His tone is just as serious as his expression.

"You can't call dibs on me washing your cucumber."

"I just did." He smirks.

"Fine. Do you like it like this?" I swirl my hand up and down the phallic vegetable, paying extra attention to my movements to purposefully torture him.

He lets out a ragged groan. "Fuck. Okay, I give up. Just please stop."

When he reaches down to adjust himself, I can't help my greedy eyes from following the movement. Damn, what I wouldn't give for a ride on that love stick. My inner muscles tingle.

"I wasn't kidding when I said it had been a while," he adds, his tone frustrated.

"It's not like I've been riding the bologna pony either,

but you don't see me getting turned on by a vegetable."
I look down at the object in question. *Hmm . . . the girth is nice. Ew, wait. What am I doing?*

"Tell me again why doing the nasty would be a bad idea?" Hayden asks.

I force myself to focus, setting the cucumber onto the wood chopping block and starting to cut it into neat slices. "Because. You're a man-whore jerkoff. And I'm pretty sure my vagina fell off after my last disaster of a relationship."

"That doesn't sound good." He turns to me with a look of concern. "Let me check things out for you down there. You know, just to make sure you're healthy."

I hold up my hand, the one with the chef's knife, and he takes an uneasy step back. "I agreed to dinner, not a vagina inspection," I remind him. I'm flushed and too warm, and hoping he doesn't notice the heat crawling up my neck. One of us has to be the strong one here.

"Fine, have it your way." He sounds genuinely disappointed, even though I thought our banter was just a little lighthearted fun.

Taking a deep breath, I continue my work as I remind myself of all the reasons Hayden and I can't go fuck like rabbits in his bed right now. Because, holy hell . . . the sight of him adjusting his hardening cock? My panties are damp and sticking to me right now. It's fucking distracting. I inhale deeply again, trying to clear my head like we do in yoga, but this time it fails to work. What have I gotten myself into?

"Dinner will be ready in about twenty minutes. You can start studying if you want," Hayden says, pulling me from my not-so-innocent thoughts.

"Sure." I gather up my materials and plant myself at his dining room table. I've just opened my laptop when the sound of him humming snaps my concentration like a twig. I look at him, watching him move effortlessly around his kitchen. God, he's adorable.

"Hey, Emery," he calls out.

"Yeah?"

He glances over at me from where he's positioned in front of the stove, stirring a pot of something. "So your mom never remarried?" Since he met my mom, we haven't spoken much about her, other than the obligatory *she was nice* type of comment he provided after.

"Nope," I say. "After my dad passed away, she had to work three jobs just to keep us in our house. That was very important to her, but left her little time for dating. She had a few boyfriends over the years, but nothing serious."

He nods along, continuing to stir. "Damn. Three jobs. I can see where you get your work ethic."

"Yes, but when I was in high school I started realizing what her sacrifices were doing to her, and I made her sell the house and cut down on her work schedule. Her body couldn't handle it anymore. After fifteen years of burning the candle at both ends, she was starting to have health problems. We moved into an apartment, and she still lives there. Keeps my room exactly the same."

When I look up from my laptop screen, he's grinning at me. "That's sweet. You have a very good mom."

"Yes, I know." Her warning rings in my head again. The one about Hayden. *Don't put stock into what'll never be.*

Taking a deep breath, I force my gaze back to my laptop screen, losing myself in the legal terms I'm studying, where things are either black or white, right or wrong, and I immediately feel at ease.

Chapter Thirteen

Hayden

I still can't believe I'm in Omaha.

Through some mix-up at the front desk, Emery and I ended up sharing a hotel room. Her room is paid for by her company, and I have no problem footing the bill for my own, but I didn't say a word; I just nodded and smiled when the clerk handed me the key card. I felt like I'd won the damn lottery. Like some tide had shifted, turning in my favor.

I'm not about to fuck with destiny. I've been jacking off to the thought of Emery for the past month. My damn hand is tired and my cock is almost raw. Maybe this time away will change things between us. I just have to decide if I want them to.

After we checked in to the hotel, Emery took off for a business meeting downstairs in one of the conference rooms while I stepped out and explored Omaha. There isn't much to see, which is why I'm already back and seated at the hotel bar with a bottle of imported beer in front of me.

I glance down to check the time on my phone. I have another thirty minutes before I'm supposed to meet Emery for a business dinner in the hotel's one restaurant—fittingly, a steakhouse. If there's one thing they've got in Nebraska, it's cows. I went over to check out the restaurant earlier, wanting to make sure they'll have a vegetarian option for her.

Plus I was just bored. I have my laptop, and I logged on to check on some properties and reply to work e-mails, but I'm unaccustomed to being out of my own city and am too restless to concentrate on work.

I wonder if this is what Emery's transition to LA has felt like? If so, I give her even more credit for how well she's handled things. I glance at my phone again. Twenty-nine more minutes.

Fuck.

• • •

Thirty-five minutes later, I'm standing in the private dining room of the restaurant, talking to a junior associate named Donald Kemp and his wife, Tabitha or Tracey, I can't remember. He's about as exciting as a wet towel. My eyes keep wandering over to the set of French doors, hungry for the first sight of her. *Where is she?*

Finally Emery floats in on a pair of high heels that make her legs seem to go on forever. And my heart rate trips over itself in a race to catch up.

She's in a cocktail dress. Classic. Black. Little spaghetti straps delicately resting on her shoulders. Her yoga-toned legs are something I've rarely gotten a glimpse of since she's usually in jeans or a business suit, and they live up to the very high standard set in my many dirty fantasies.

I open my mouth to excuse myself from Donald when an older man with floppy gray hair and a bad set of veneers approaches Emery, placing his hand on her waist and leaning in to tell her something. She cringes.

Murderous rage boils inside me and I want to deck the son of a bitch. Clenching my fists at my sides, I excuse myself and stride over toward her. Thoughts of pissing on her leg, like a dog does with a hydrant, to mark my territory flash through my mind. *Shit.* I can't do that to Emery. Stopping beside her, my eyes land on Mr. Pudgy, Gray, and Slimy.

"Hayden, this is Mr. Pratt, my *boss* at the firm," Emery says pointedly, obviously sensing my murderous attitude and trying to calm me down. "And this is Hayden Oliver. He's a real-estate developer."

"It's nice to meet you," I bite out in a clipped tone.

Mr. Pratt nods, and I wonder if this is Larry The Creeper she's told me about. Most likely she has a couple of bosses at the firm, but a gut feeling tells me this is the head honcho.

"Emery's doing phenomenal work. It's a pleasure having her, as I'm sure you know," he says, giving me a sly wink that makes my stomach turn.

Doesn't this guy realize he's old enough to be Emery's father? *Ick.* No wonder she's sworn off men. Then again, now that I've met Emery's mother, there's no way she'd stand for a douche-nozzle like this guy. I've discovered where Emery gets her no-nonsense attitude.

"By the way, call me Larry," The Creeper says, leaning in toward me. His breath is a mix of rancid mayonnaise and week-old bologna. *Gag.*

Taking a step closer to Emery, I tug her away from his grabby hands and closer to me. Her eyes widen and meet mine.

I lean down to whisper near her ear, letting my lips touch her neck just slightly. "I'll behave. I just don't want him touching you."

She gives me a tight nod, her eyes darting between mine and his. It's clear she doesn't want to get in the middle of the standoff happening between me and her boss. But I sense she's grateful to be away from him just the same.

I guide Emery over toward the bar. "Something to drink?" I ask, my voice calmer once we're away from her foul boss.

"Please." Her eyes plead with mine, and I can sense that whatever happened today, it was a hell of a day.

"Something strong. But not too strong," she adds.

I scan the drink menu and motion the bartender over. "A red sangria, please." It's made with a nice cabernet and a splash of orange liqueur, so it'll be a little stronger than plain wine, but not strong enough that she'll be tempted to act undignified in front of her colleagues. And with the sliced oranges and cherries as a garnish, it's fun and girly without being obnoxious.

When I turn to hand her the drink, she beams at me.

"Thank you. That's perfect."

I place my hand at the small of her back, the strange need to be close to her flashing through me.

Once Emery has her drink and she's taken a few sips, I can see her begin to relax. Her shoulders drop by about two inches and her mouth relaxes into a welcoming grin. I bet there are knots in her back and neck that I could work out later . . . but I'm getting ahead of myself.

Finally, we sit down for dinner. I pull out a chair for Emery, only to watch Asshat Larry slide into the seat next to hers. I have to lean down and ask one of her colleagues if he minds trading seats with me so that I can sit beside her. Many of the associate attorneys have brought their wives. In fact, the only person riding solo is Larry.

I seriously want to kick her creepy-ass boss in the nut sack. I don't like the way he's been looking at her in her cocktail dress all evening, and weaseling his way in to sit next to her is just weird.

At least everyone at our table is in a celebratory mood. They won a settlement today that's been two years in the making. Tomorrow will be about tying up loose ends, signing the contracts, and working out the small details. Emery contributed, despite being new and young, and her boss is impressed with her. So that's a silver lining.

We make small talk, the conversation often turning toward technical minutiae and office politics that Emery navigates with ease. I love watching her in action, sparring with these men twice her age. It's pretty incredible. Finally, the waitstaff scurries out with steaming silver trays, ready to serve dinner.

"What the hell is this?" Larry looks down at Emery's

plate, which contains grilled veggies and pasta in wine sauce—exactly what I ordered for her when I came to the restaurant earlier and learned the menu for our dinner party had already been selected, without taking her preferences into consideration. "Someone get this girl a steak," he demands, glaring at the waitstaff.

"No, Mr. Pratt . . . I mean Larry," Emery says. "It's fine."

I lean in toward him. "She's a vegetarian. I made sure she'd be taken care of tonight."

Her gaze darts over to mine and a grateful look crosses her features. Something tells me if I hadn't intervened tonight, she'd be stuck eating a few spears of broccoli for dinner, and I'm not okay with that. I get that she wants to make a good impression with the senior partners, but damn, she should be able to eat what she likes.

"A vegetarian?" Larry scoffs.

I'm not sure how he didn't know that information. Emery's been working with him for a month. I distinctly recall her setting me straight about that when we first met. Then again, maybe she's just more comfortable with me.

I dig into my steak while Emery, seemingly pleased, swirls pasta on her fork and shovels a big bite into her mouth. She eats with gusto, with none of the fake, coy dieting crap that some girls pull. *Oh, I've had one lettuce leaf—I'm full.*

As I tune out the dry conversation about mergers and acquisitions happening around me, I notice little things about Emery during dinner. The way her simple gold necklace rests against the dip in her delicate collarbone. The way her dark eyelashes flutter against her cheeks when she looks down. The sound of her laughter when she lets loose—it's a throaty sound, and I find I like it way more than is normal.

Generally with women, I have the finesse and mental fortitude of a rhinoceros charging through a watering hole. With Emery, I want to catalog every little detail. I could stare at her for hours. The way she dabs her cloth napkin at her mouth, so as not to mess up her lipstick. It's cute.

When dinner is through, I make my way over to the bar, needing one more drink if I'm to survive the rest of this evening. I've just ordered a Scotch on the rocks when Larry saunters over. The piece of broccoli between his front teeth is so large, it practically requires its own zip code. Of course, I don't say a word.

"It's good to hear today went well," I say, mentally checking *Make small talk* off my to-do list. I'm about to wander away when Larry turns to face me, pinning me against the bar.

"How long have you and Emery been dating, son?"

"Oh, we're just friends," I say, correcting him.

Larry raises one bushy gray brow. "She said she was bringing her boyfriend."

"Did she?" I ask with more than a hint of curiosity in my tone.

Larry nods, the broccoli between his teeth waggling at me. "She did."

"Excuse me," I say and head straight over to Emery,

tearing her away from one of her colleagues. Dick, or Bob, or whatever.

She glares at me, nearly tripping over her high-heeled feet as I pull her to a quiet side of the room. "What's gotten into you? Did you tell Larry I was your boyfriend?"

I'm not sure why, but my tone is dripping with annoyed frustration. I haven't been labeled anyone's boyfriend since . . . yeah. After which, a state of emergency was declared upon my life, and things have never been quite the same.

Planting one hand on her hip, her posture straightens. "Aren't you?"

All of our time spent together over the past month comes crashing into me at once, like starbursts firing in my synapses. The casual meals we've shared, the easy conversations, me lacing my fingers between hers, tucking loose strands of hair behind her ear and fantasizing about her. *God, the fucking fantasies I've had . . .*

My jaw tenses. Maybe this whole thing is my fault. One big, huge colossal mess. But it all felt right. More than right. Perfect, actually. It's been easy and fun—in a way that it never has been when it comes to the women in my life.

Emery's still waiting for me to answer, so I do the only thing I can think of. I lean down and take her mouth with mine. Her hands fly to the lapels of my suit jacket, and for a second, I think she's going to push me away. But then she tugs me closer and groans into my mouth. Gripping her waist tightly, I devour her just like I've fantasized about for so long. My tongue strokes hers in long licks as little mewling sounds escape her. I want to strip her right here and fuck her against the wall, bounce her up and down on my cock while her boss watches.

My dick is already rock hard. *Fuck.*

"We've got to get out of here," I say in a low voice, practically panting.

"Yes," she agrees, just as breathless.

Taking her hand, I pull her from the restaurant and down the hall toward the elevators. I consider pulling her into the stairwell—it's closer than our room—but not nearly private enough for what I want to do to her.

Jabbing the button with my finger, I don't release my hold on Emery's hand. Finally the doors open and we step inside, joining an elderly couple who nod and smile at us. But then Granny's eyes travel down to the large bulge at the front of my pants, and she takes a step back.

"Oh my," she says, her hand flying to her mouth.

Emery giggles and buries her face into my neck. The warm puff of her breath against my skin sends tingling heat down my spine and into my groin, making my dick even harder.

"Not helping, sweetheart," I murmur. I want to swat her ass, but in the presence of our audience, I resist. Just barely.

The elevator stops at our floor and we make a hasty exit. Emery stumbles, tipsy from the three sangrias she's had, and lets me tug her down the hall.

Finally we're inside our room, and when the door closes behind us, the only sound is of our thumping heartbeats. The room is dim, except for the bathroom light that was left on, creating a swath of light to see by.

"Why'd you tell Larry I was your boyfriend?" I ask, my voice a mere whisper.

"You saw how he is with me."

"Yeah." I roll my eyes. "I wanted to fucking hit him in the face. Repeatedly."

"I couldn't come here and be the only one without a date. I needed you."

"As a buffer," I say.

She nods, reluctantly. "Do you mind?"

"No, actually. It's cool. But why not say we were just friends, you know, tell the truth?"

She swallows and looks down at the carpeting. "Sometimes it feels like . . ."

"More," I say, finishing for her.

Her gaze flies up to mine. "Yeah."

I take a deep shaky breath, not knowing what to say

next. This whole situation is my fault.

"But I know you don't want that," she says, her voice small.

"I want you," I tell her, lifting her chin to look at me.

Alarm bells ring in my head. Beth's warnings, Hudson's lectures . . . but all of it means nothing. Because I want her. So badly it hurts.

Her hand dips down and she grips my cock through my pants. "Yeah, I picked up on that."

A grunt of surprise pushes past my lips as she rubs her hand up and down. "Fuck."

"You're not fit to take out in public. Scaring women and children like that." She makes a *tsking* sound.

"What are you going to do about it, Miss Winters?"

I lean down and take her mouth again. Damn, one hit and I'm addicted to her. She lets me devour her mouth, her warm tongue stroking mine as I grind my erection into her soft belly.

Letting out a loud gasp, Emery breaks away from our

kiss.

"What?" I ask.

"I'm sure you were lying about that whole nine-inches thing, but I have to know." Her grin turns devilish as her hands move to my zipper, and she slowly tugs it down.

I lace my fingers and cross my hands behind my head as I lean back against the wall. "Have at it, babe."

She smirks at me and then goes back to work, reaching inside my black boxer briefs. I feel her warm palm curl around me, and it's heaven.

She grips me and pulls out my cock. "Holy shit."

"What?" I look down to see her view.

We're both fully clothed, with just my cock between us. Her hand doesn't even close around my girth, but it's such a pretty sight—her manicured red nails and delicate hand holding me this way.

"Women actually let you put this thing inside them?"

I want to laugh at her innocence, but I don't. "Come here," I say, leaning down to kiss her again.

I want her to stroke that pretty little hand up and down—I'm so fucking worked up that I'm ready to explode, but I don't want to rush her. I know this is a huge moment for us. There might be no going back to being friends after this, and I have no idea what that means, or how to process it. I only know that I want her underneath me, on top of me, everywhere.

Reaching behind her, I unzip her dress and let it fall to the floor. She's wearing a black strapless bra that pushes her titties up so nice and high for me to admire, and little black boy shorts. Practical, comfortable, but still sexy as hell. My hands skim down her body, over the dip in her waist and down to her ass, where her round cheeks peek from the undies she's wearing.

Finally her hand begins working up and down. It feels good.

"Use two hands, baby," I encourage her. She giggles but adds a second hand, and fuck, now that feels *really* good.

When I rub my thumb over the front of her panties,

Emery releases a little grunt of pleasure. I want to make her come. I want to take her over to the bed. But instead, I switch our positions so she's the one leaning up against the wall, braced with support. Then I push my fingers inside her panties and find her soaking wet. Her little pearl of a clit is already swollen and distended, as if reaching out for me. I circle it with my finger and Emery moans.

"Hayden. Oh God."

"You like me touching this hot little pussy?" I whisper, speeding up my strokes.

She cries out and rubs her greedy hands up and down my cock while her hips press forward, giving me all the access I want to her wet cunt.

"Hayden," she says on a groan. "What are we doing?"

I look at her—really look at her—and realize she's tipsy. And questioning what we're doing. I suddenly feel like a grade-A asshole. She's not sure about this, and my determination instantly fades.

"Emery. I'm sorry," I murmur, taking a step back and

tucking myself into my pants. *Ouch. Damn zipper.* I have to stop this before we go too far . . . do something we'll both regret in the morning.

"W-what?" she asks, her eyes glassy and her cheeks pink. "What are you doing?"

"You've had too much to drink. You're not thinking clearly, and I wouldn't want to take advantage."

She takes a step toward me, her chest bouncing in the push-up bra. "You're not . . ."

I lean down and press my lips to hers. "It's just not a good idea. Good night."

I'm not sure when I turned so chivalrous, but I take a deep breath and force myself to walk away. Since we're sharing a room, the only reprieve is the bathroom—and that's where I go. I pull out my aching cock and jack it so hard and fast, I'm almost raw by the time I come.

When I'm composed and cleaned up, I exit the bathroom and find Emery already curled up in bed, lying on her side, facing away from me as she snores lightly.

And I know I've made the right decision.

At least, I hope I have.

Chapter Fourteen

Emery

Yet another endless day of negotiations and legal nitpicking. The hotel's air-conditioning can barely keep the stifling atmosphere at bay.

I resist the urge to drum my fingers on the polished conference table. *For Christ's sake, you indecisive twits . . . what the hell is the problem?* These suit-wearing chimps said they were happy with the paperwork when we e-mailed them our final drafts two weeks ago. Why did they wait until now to start hemming and hawing and scribbling notes?

These documents should be signed, sealed, and delivered already. I thought we were done with this freaking case. Isn't that why we all flew out to the middle of nowhere? What happened to all that "celebrate a job well done" stuff? Even on a good day, this dull-as-dishwater meeting would make me antsy . . . and my memories of last night elevate it to pure torture.

I can't stop thinking about the skillful way that Hayden kisses. His long, thick cock tenting his pants and throbbing in my hands. His deft fingers on my clit. He looks incredibly handsome in a suit, but now I know that he looks even better halfway out of one. I wonder how he would look completely naked. Probably like a sculpture from ancient Greece. Why do I have to be stuck in here? Why isn't that sexy bastard on top of me right now?

Fuck . . . I'm slowly but surely driving myself insane. I wish Hayden hadn't stopped our fun just before we got to the good part. Sure, I was buzzed, but I wasn't *that* drunk.

Unable to fight off my horny boredom anymore, I hide my phone under the table and text him as subtly as possible.

EMERY: *Please kill me now.*

A minute later, my phone vibrates.

HAYDEN: Sorry, no can do. Would a good joke help?

My heart races as I text back.

EMERY: The only thing that would make this meeting less awful is if you were under the table.

I try to quell my nerves. Will he take the bait? Will my flirting come across as sexy or desperate? Maybe I shouldn't have done that. If I have to, I can always pass it off as a joke.

My trepidation dissolves into a flush of heat at his near-immediate reply.

HAYDEN: Fuck yes. I've thought about that.

I fight to avoid cracking a smile in front of the fat cats.

EMERY: *Why am I not surprised?*

HAYDEN: *Because you're at the office all the time, looking like a hot librarian. A man's fantasies have to come from somewhere.*

EMERY: *Thanks for the insight into your creative process, Mr. Oliver.*

I bite my lip at his next message.

HAYDEN: *I'd hide under your desk, my head under your skirt. Reward the high-powered lawyer for all her hard work. Suck on your clit until you were nice an*

d wet for me. Could you keep a straight face if someone came in?

This really isn't helping me sit still and pay attention, but I can't bring myself to stop now. My body is running on pure adrenaline now.

EMERY: *Nope, that's why we'd lock the door.*

Too aroused to be embarrassed, I add: *If you did a good job, I'd let you fuck me on my desk.*

HAYDEN: *I always do a good job.*

EMERY: *Is that so? I'm sure you could provide a long list of references.*

HAYDEN: *What can I say? This level of skill takes practice.*

My lip quirks in amusement at his cockiness. A few weeks ago, his tendency to fuck everything that moved would have bothered me—especially if he didn't even try to deny it. But I've accepted his checkered past as part of him. Nobody's perfect, after all. And it's not like we're dating. We're just two friends who want to fool around.

After a few more rounds of borderline sexting, he changes the subject.

> HAYDEN: *What's your schedule for tonight? I want to steal you away.*

My stomach flips with excitement.

> EMERY: *Promise I'll be done by six. Meet you at the hotel bar?*

> HAYDEN: *Wouldn't miss it for the world.*

I slip my phone back into my purse, feeling self-satisfied. I've made my decision: I'm going to sleep with him tonight. No more second-guessing my own judgment, no more obsessing over what the future might bring, no more vaguely moralistic *oh, I really shouldn't* waffling.

I'm a grown-ass woman; there's nothing wrong with going out and fulfilling my needs. We're both single and horny. We both want this . . . dear God, do we ever want it. Now that I've had a taste of Hayden, I won't rest until I get the whole main course. I want to seize the moment—along with a few other more solid things.

A little whiny voice in my head questions: *Even if it ruins our friendship?* I firmly tell my superego to shut its nonexistent pie hole. One night of sex won't ruin anything. People have fuck buddies and friends with benefits all the time. It's clearly not impossible. Whatever the hell our relationship is now—whatever it will become—we can make it work.

Methinks the lady doth protest too much, whispers the voice. *If you have to try this hard to convince yourself . . .*

But the mental image of a very naked, very erect Hayden quiets it right down. My core clenches and I have to press my thighs together under the conference table. Guilt and anxiety can't last a minute against my need to get laid. It's been way too long, and by God, I've earned this. I can practically feel that huge cock filling me already.

I shift in my chair as discreetly as I can manage, already slick and aching between my thighs. This is going to be a long damn afternoon.

• • •

That evening at five minutes after six, I hurry into the hotel lobby's bar to find Hayden already perched at a high-top table for two. He's sipping from a tumbler of amber whiskey on the rocks; in front of the other chair sits what looks like a peach Bellini in a frosty glass. Another one of my favorite cocktails. It's a cute gesture, but right now, I'm not sure if I want to take the time to drink it.

"Sorry I'm late," I call out as I walk over, putting a little extra swish in my hips. *Never let it be said that Emery Winters has forgotten how to get a man's attention.*

His eyes fall on me and ignite like coals. "Hey, you." The low note of promise in his voice warms me from the inside out. And his smile is a slow, wonderful curl of lips that reminds me of all the things he texted me earlier. All the things he wanted to do with that sinful mouth . . .

I lean over the table to taste him in a feverish kiss. He reacts instantly, one hand falling to my hip and the other tangling in my hair, pulling me closer. He nips at my lower lip and I let out a soft moan, my arousal renewing itself with a throb.

We really shouldn't be playing tonsil hockey in public like this. I already want to push him against the wall, like he did to me last night, or let him throw me onto the floor. If he keeps doing that *thing* with his tongue, we might end up getting the cops called on us. But, *mmm*, handcuffs . . . that might be fun too.

As I pull back for a breath, the dark hunger in Hayden's eyes almost hauls me right back in like a gravitational force. But the mood deflates a little when I see Mr. Pratt over Hayden's shoulder, paused at the bar entrance to stare at us. He looks totally bewildered.

Hayden glances back for a moment. "Oh . . . right. He must be confused as shit."

"Why's that?" I ask in an amused tone that's more like

What did you do?

"I may have told him that I'm completely, definitely not your boyfriend."

The implications sink in and I laugh out loud. Now that I think about it, I did see them talking on the other side of the ballroom last night, didn't I? Mr. Pratt must have been the one to prompt Hayden's freak-out. And Hayden insisted that we were just friends—right before he rushed over to suck my face off. Nothing confusing about that.

Poor little Larry The Creeper probably has no clue what's going on anymore. Well, it's none of his fucking business.

Just to rub it in, I lean into Hayden for another long, deep kiss. I don't need the label of "boyfriend" with him. All I need is his skilled mouth and his muscled body pressed against mine. When I finally pull my mouth from his, a glance up tells me that Larry is still there. Still watching us. I grimace.

Hayden glances toward Larry and his jaw twitches.

"Great. I'm going to have to kill that man now." A soft, wistful sigh follows, and I decide my very favorite thing about Hayden—well, other than his big dick and deep kisses—is his sense of humor. That and his protectiveness.

"With your bare hands?" I ask hopefully.

"Undoubtedly."

"To protect my innocence?" I bat my eyelashes, playing along in a way I hope is sexy.

Tracing my jaw with his thumb and pulling me closer, Hayden is a fraction away from kissing me again. "Something tells me you're not so innocent. You like to fuck dirty, don't you?"

A surprised little gasp escapes me, and Hayden quiets the sound with his mouth, kissing me hard again. Then he breaks away and glances over my shoulder. "He's gone. And probably thoroughly fucking confused. But hopefully he won't bother you too much anymore."

Despite his playboy lifestyle and occasional closed-off moments, I know Hayden cares for me. He's been nothing but sweet and fun for our entire friendship.

And yesterday, he was practically a knight in shining armor. He made polite small talk with my coworkers, even though I'm sure he was bored out of his mind. He warded off Larry The Creeper without making a scene. He went out of his way to make sure I got a decent vegetarian dinner—in a steakhouse, no less. He toughed out what must have been an epic case of blue balls just because I was tipsy.

Overall, he seems like the total package. An attentive, handsome guy who's seen me at my most graceless and still thinks I'm the best thing since sliced bread. He can even guess my favorite drinks, for Christ's sake. That's good enough for me. More than enough. Isn't it?

Focus on the pros, Emery . . . they far outweigh the cons. I let a sultry smile curve my lips. *Remember what you came here for. Why rock the boat when you can rock the bed?*

This time, Hayden is the one to pull back before things get too R-rated for public display. "I talked to the hotel concierge," he says casually, as if he weren't hiding a huge boner under the table. "He recommended some fun touristy things to do in Omaha. It's kind of a short list, but there's an art museum, a botanical garden, a community theater. They're performing *Annie* at seven tonight . . . an off-Broadway rendition." He chuckles. "Way the hell off."

I cover his hand with mine. "Let's just go back to the room," I say, looking deep into his gorgeous blue eyes.

He blinks in surprise. From the subtle breath he draws in, I can tell he knows exactly what I want and how badly I want it. And he's dying to give it to me. "What about dinner?" he asks, offering me one last chance to back out and pretend none of this ever happened.

No fucking way, babe. You're mine tonight. "We can order room service," I reply. My thumb rubs the back of his hand in slow circles. "After."

His grin turns absolutely devilish. That's all the confirmation I need.

Abandoning our drinks in their sweat rings on the table, we pay our bar tab and make a break for it. We hurry toward the elevator like a pair of teenagers who finally have the house to themselves.

My stomach jitters with eager butterflies. There are no nosy colleagues or scandalized old ladies to slow us down this time. No cocktail buzz to guilt Hayden into leaving me alone again. In fact, I can't think when I last felt more sober; I'm so awake, so alive, my skin is sparking with desire. I almost can't stand the anticipation as the elevator slowly dings its way up to our floor. I want his hands on me and his cock inside me right this second.

With his longer stride, Hayden reaches our room door first. He opens it for me with a flourish and a hungry gleam in his eye. "Ladies first."

He squeezes my ass as I walk through, and I squeak with surprise, giggling. I'm acting like a giddy schoolgirl and I couldn't care less.

But when the heavy door clicks shut behind us, I can't help but pause. As soaking wet as my panties are, as much as every part of me wants Hayden . . . sex is such a big step. Who could charge over a cliff like this without even hesitating at the edge? As much as I've tried to convince myself that sleeping together is no big deal, it's going to have ripple effects. No way around that.

When I turn to look at him, Hayden's expression has softened, concern shining through his desire. I realize that my apprehension is contagious. He knows as well as I do that this is it. We're about to have sex—and our friendship will never be quite the same again. Even if that change is for the better, it'll still take some getting used to. Is Hayden willing to work through the awkward stage that's coming? I'm not even sure if *I'm* ready for it.

But then again, is anyone ever completely ready for anything new? Life happens at its own pace. I can't make this leap smaller or less intimidating by worrying about it. Either I back away and spend the rest of my life wondering what could have been . . . or I take the plunge.

Right now.

Chapter Fifteen

Hayden

Emery stands in the center of our hotel room, her wide blue eyes locked on mine, looking apprehensive. After dirty-texting all day, I've been wound up and horny, so when she sauntered into the hotel bar, dressed in a black pencil skirt and white button-down top, looking ever so prim and proper, I wanted to strip her down and fuck her senseless. Now . . . I'm not so sure.

"Hey, come here," I say, holding out my hand. She crosses the room toward me, placing her shaky palm in mine. "We don't have to do this. We don't have to do anything you're not ready for." All the confidence and bravado she had downstairs has faded away.

"Sorry, it's just nerves."

"It's okay, Emery." My tone is soft and reassuring, but inside my hormones are raging and my body is on fire. "It was probably a stupid idea."

She chews on her lower lip, her eyes fixed on mine. She's lost in thought—she's always thinking, but for just once, I wish she wouldn't. "No. I'm sorry, I'm a little nervous. It's just that I haven't done this in a while. But I want to."

Hearing her say those words, my pulse riots. "I'll go slow. Just tell me if you want me to stop."

She gives me a tight nod, and her shoulders relax.

"Come here." I tug her to the bed and we sit down on the edge of it. I've never put this much thought into sex or seduction before, but I know I need to calm her down and get her ready, or this night's going to be over before it even starts.

"What are you doing?" she asks, watching me curiously.

"We could talk first," I suggest. I haven't even asked her about her day.

She chuckles. "Somehow I don't think that will help."

"Right." I run my hand along the back of my neck. "Elephant in the room and all that."

She nods.

"I have an idea," I say, rising from the bed. "Unbutton your top. I'll be right back."

Curiosity flashes in her eyes, but her fingers go to work on the buttons as I walk into the bathroom and grab a bottle of the hotel-supplied body lotion. I dump some into my palms and rub my hands together to warm it.

"A massage," I say. "To relax you."

Emery smiles and pulls her white shirt from her shoulders, tossing it on the floor. With the scent of mint and lavender hanging in the air around us, she lies down on the bed on her belly, her head to the side so her eyes are still on mine.

"Thanks for this, Hayden," she says when my hands make contact with her skin.

I knead her stiff shoulders, pressing my thumbs between her shoulder blades to work out the knots I find. "Not a problem."

I lose myself in the process, touching her shapely shoulders that I've admired for all these weeks. Pushing my fingers in along her spine until she's nice and relaxed. She murmurs and lets out little grunts of satisfaction that are sexy as hell. I unclasp her bra and let the straps fall to the sides so I can continue rubbing her without the restrictive material in the way. Getting lost in my movements and her little groans, I realize I'm straddling her, my cock nestled against her ass cheeks, while my hips seem to be rocking against her on their own.

"Let me up," she says, her tone suddenly stern.

Shit. I rise up onto my knees, and Emery lifts up too. I expect her to cover her chest with her hands, or to yell at me for being so presumptuous when I said it was only a massage.

But instead, she turns around on the bed so she's facing me. Her chest is heaving wildly with heavy breaths and her skin is flushed. I can't resist letting my eyes wander from hers. *Beautiful.* Her breasts are full and perky, with soft pink nipples that have puckered in the cool air-conditioning.

She's looking at me hungrily, her eyes jumping between mine to where my cock is straining against my pants. In a heartbeat, everything has changed between us.

"Are you sure you're ready for this?" I ask.

She nods, biting her lip.

"Tell me."

"I want it," she whispers, inching her way closer to where I'm kneeling on the bed. As she brings her hands to my belt, her eyes stay locked on mine. "It's all I thought about all day."

"Me too," I admit. Sending dirty texts all afternoon has left my libido in high gear. All systems are primed and ready to go. I must seek and plunder.

Undoing my pants, Emery works one hand into the front of my boxer briefs. My cock hardens even more as I feel her hand curl around me. I lean forward and take her mouth with mine. Once we begin, there's no awkward fumbling, no hesitation. Her hand strokes up and down while I suck her tongue into my mouth and fondle the prettiest set of tits I've ever seen. When my thumbs graze her nipples, Emery moans and breaks from my mouth.

"Do you have any condoms?"

I nod. "'Course. I'm like a Boy Scout."

She grins, pushing my boxers and pants down my thighs.

"But you're getting ahead of yourself. I already told you I wanted to eat that sweet pussy of yours."

She lets out a little groan, trailing her fingernails along my shaft and down to my balls. Goose bumps break out along my thighs. *Christ, I want her.*

"Is this going to change things between us?" she asks.

Ah. The real reason she went from horny to apprehensive in three seconds flat. "You're really going to ask me that when your hand is on my cock?" *And expect an honest answer*, I want to add, but don't. I meet her eyes and see fear and desire and confusion buried in those wide blue depths. "It doesn't have to. Friends 'til the end. Okay?"

She nods, lifting her delicate chin and still holding my eyes.

I'm not some douchebag who's going to lie to her and promise her the world. This is me. This is what I can offer her. She blinks and nods again, seeming to make up her mind. Then her fist around me relaxes. I give her shoulders a little push so she's sitting back against the bed. After pulling down the zipper of her pencil skirt, she lifts her hips when I give her skirt and panties a tug. Soon she's naked, and I take a moment just to appreciate the view.

"Damn," I murmur.

"What?" She looks down at herself.

"I'd say yoga paid off."

She's soft like a woman should be, but her stomach is flat and her thighs are toned. She's perfect. And shaved bare—which I didn't expect, revealing delicate pink pussy lips that I want to part and bury my tongue against.

Giggling, she swats my shoulder. I rise from the bed and ditch the rest of my clothes before I push her thighs apart and position myself between them.

"This isn't going to be like with Fuckstick or whoever. If you don't like what I'm doing, or you need me to change pressure or speed, you're going to tell me. You're going to tug on my hair and tell me to the left, or harder, or whatever you need to climax. Do you understand?"

She nods, smiling at me.

"Promise?"

I hate how some women would rather fake an orgasm with high-pitched squeals rather than just tell their partner, *Dude, suck on my clit until I scream your name.* It's really not that hard, but guys can be dense assholes sometimes.

She nods again.

The goal is to make her feel like she's in control. I've gotten to know her these past few weeks, and I know that she's the type to overthink everything and get lost inside her head. If I make sure she knows she's the one calling the shots, that'll be less likely to happen.

Pushing her legs open just a little wider, I lean down and lick my way from top to bottom, tasting her and breathing her in. Emery squirms, and I have to grip her hips to hold her in place. I center my mouth right over her sensitive nub and flick my tongue up and down until I feel her body shaking.

Then I devour her, sucking and licking until she's a trembling, screaming mess. Shouting out my name, she loses that perfect control, coming hard against my face. I immediately want to do that again. But first I have bigger priorities. My cock has been neglected for way too long, and I need to rectify that. I grab a condom from my duffel bag that's sitting beside the bed, and rip open the package with my teeth.

"Let me," Emery says, sitting up and taking it from my hands.

Ever so carefully, she sheaths me, slowly unrolling the condom all the way down my shaft. I've never had a woman do this, and it feels way more erotic than it should. Once she's satisfied with a job well done, she looks up at me, her cheeks flushed from her earlier orgasm and her eyes shining.

I lean forward and press a kiss to her reddened lips. "I've wanted to fuck you since we first met," I admit.

"Come on then, big boy." I feel her smile against my mouth.

Positioning my body over hers, I line my cock up with her entrance and rub the head of it back and forth through her wetness, teasing her.

"God, I can't wait to see what you feel like," I admit.

"And I can't wait to see if you really know where the G-spot is."

I almost chuckle to myself, almost, but then Emery wraps her legs around my ass and grinds against me, pushing her wet pussy up and down my shaft, and I forget how to breathe, let alone laugh.

"Goddamn it, hold still," I mutter.

With one forearm holding up my weight over her, I use my other hand to grip the base of my cock and slowly feed it into her. Inch by tight inch, her body accepts mine.

Fuck. That feels good. Finally, I'm buried within her and I press my hips close to hers, savoring the feeling of being sheathed in her warmth.

"You're really fucking tight," I say with a grunt. When I look down, I see Emery's eyes squeezed shut and she's biting her lip. "Are you okay?"

She gives a nod of approval. "Yeah. It's just . . . been a while."

"Take a deep breath," I say, retreating a few inches.

She sucks a big breath into her lungs, and her body, while still tense and clutching at me, relaxes just a little.

"That's it. Now hang on."

Emery brings her hands to my shoulders while I begin pumping in earnest. Soon, Emery's moaning and digging in her heels against my ass as she grinds herself even closer on every down stroke. She feels so incredible that I lose myself in her, thrusting hard and fast, cursing under my breath as I press my lips against her neck.

I'm not sure if sex has ever been this good, and I never want it to end.

Chapter Sixteen

Emery

Hayden moves with the certainty of a man who knows what he's doing. His lips crash against mine and my pulse skitters wildly. The room is filled with the sounds of our flesh slapping together.

I cry out and clutch his biceps for support as the most intense orgasm of my life hits me. This is the third he's wrung from my body in the last hour, and I feel as if I'm floating on cloud nine. The man can fuck, there's no denying that. It's like he has a damn map of my vagina, the G-spot charted out in big block letters: PLEASURE CENTRAL—RIGHT HERE!

Little droplets of sweat dot along the back of his neck; I feel dampness when I lace my fingers behind his head and pull him down for a kiss. His lips move tenderly with mine as the urgency of our fucking slows down to a softer pace. He has such control, such stamina, but I think he's finally getting close. His cock thickens inside me and he groans softly near my ear. It's the best sound in the whole world, knowing he's finally following me over the edge.

"Emery," he says on a groan, his teeth grazing the sensitive skin at the base of my throat.

After he comes, he keeps pumping in and out of me slowly, as if savoring the way I feel around him. When he reluctantly pulls out, he gathers me up in his arms and holds me, our limbs tangled and the sheets damp with our perspiration. I feel tired and boneless. It's perfection. Better than I knew sex could be.

"Fuck. Why did we wait so long to do that?" he asks, still breathing hard, burying his face in the crook of my neck.

"Because we're friends?" I suggest helpfully.

"Right. Totally. I'd say now we're more like best friends."

"Besties." I almost choke on the word. *Why is my heart clenching in my chest?*

As he rises from the bed and heads into the bathroom,

to get rid of the condom, I presume, I take a deep breath, trying to get a hold of myself. I feel totally confused and out of control.

What the hell was I thinking? I just had sex with Hayden Oliver. Hayden *Fucking* Oliver. The man Roxy and my mom both warned me about with pitchforks and danger signs. Well, maybe it wasn't quite that dramatic, but it was close.

I hear the faucet running in the bathroom, and I curl onto my side, hugging the pillow to my chest. It's scented like him: cologne, sweat, sex. The smell makes my pussy throb again, makes me want him in my arms and between my legs . . . even as I want to push him away so I can figure all this out.

My heart is still thumping like a jackhammer when he approaches the bed and flops down beside me.

"You okay?" he asks, looking at me with something close to concern in his eyes.

"Yeah, of course," I lie. "You?"

"Never better. That was incredible." He shoves a pillow under his head and gazes up at the ceiling. "So, meetings all day again tomorrow?" he asks, like nothing's out of the ordinary. Like we didn't just have the best sex of my life. Like my brain isn't turning itself inside out.

"Uh, yeah." I can't even think straight right now. How am I supposed to function in business meetings only eight hours from now?

"Do you still want to order room service?" Hayden asks, rolling over to face me in the dim light.

I shrug. "Not really." My appetite has vanished. Along with my common sense, apparently. "I might just turn in early."

"Cool with me," he says. "Mind if I turn on the TV? We could watch the end of the game."

I reach over to the nightstand and hand him the remote.

He kisses the top of my head and pulls me onto his chest. He's warm and solid, and I curl up like a cat, letting him hold me.

As the steady sound of his heartbeat thumps under my ear, a pit of dread churns in my stomach. I never meant to let this happen, but holy shit, I'm falling in love with him. I'm screwed—completely and utterly screwed.

And not in the fun way.

Chapter Seventeen

Hayden

In the morning, I stretch my stiff limbs and rise from the bed, then lumber into the bathroom and swing the door shut behind me. When I lift the toilet seat and begin pissing, I wonder why in the hell my cock feels funny. Like I spent all night fucking.

Then the memories start rushing back. Emery writhing beneath me. Her legs wound around my back. Our mouths fused together in hungry kisses. The tightest pussy I've ever felt milking me.

Damn. That was intense. Who knew my buttoned-up, yoga-loving lawyer would be a fucking rock star in the sack?

I want a repeat, but when I emerge from the bathroom, I can see her sleeping form still curled up in the heap of messy sheets. Knowing that she's got another big day of meetings ahead of her, I decide to let her rest a little longer.

As quietly as possible, I grab a pair of sweats from my bag and go into the adjoining living room of the suite. Flipping through the hotel's room service menu, I pick up the phone and order us breakfast and coffee, then sit down in the armchair with my cell phone.

Soon after, I hear her stir in the adjoining bedroom, soft footfalls of bare feet padding across the carpeting . . . then the distinct sound of her passing gas. Loudly.

I chuckle to myself, my mouth pulling up into a grin. The other room is totally silent until I clear my throat.

"Is there even a remote chance you didn't hear that?" she asks, peeking at me from around the corner.

Her hair is an absolute mess and there are little smudges of black makeup under her eyes. She's naked, clutching the white sheet around her chest. And her cheeks are stained bright red—presumably from embarrassment. But she still somehow looks good.

I chuckle again. "Don't worry about it. It was cute."

Her eyebrows dart up in surprise. "Cute," she repeats, sounding confused. And then she dashes off for the bathroom, and probably the shower since her meetings start in another hour from now.

I hear the spray of water and the shower curtain being pulled along the rod. Lost in thought, I'm staring at my phone reading an e-mail from Hudson when it suddenly hits me and I bolt up out of my chair.

Cute? The fuck?

My heart begins hammering in my chest, and my palms break out in a damp sweat. Hudson's words come rushing back to me. I realize that if I thought that was *cute*, my feelings for her are a lot deeper than I ever bargained for.

Picking up my phone again, I dial Hudson in a blind panic, trying not to freak the fuck out. He will explain this to me. He has to. I can't let hysteria set in. I take a deep breath, trying to calm my nerves.

"Yo," he answers. "How's Oklahoma?"

"It's Nebraska," I bark. I have no time for pleasantries. I'm dealing with a CODE RED emergency here.

"Oh, right. What's up, man?"

"She just fucking farted."

A long silent pause. "So I take it you left her?" he says with a chuckle.

"No. Worse. I thought it was cute. I laughed it off and told her not to worry about it. She was mortified, of course."

I glance to the bathroom door, which is still shut. The sound of water running tells me she's still showering.

"Okay, we'll talk this out. You can get through this," Hudson reassures me with only a hint of a mocking tone to his voice.

"Damn it. This wasn't supposed to happen."

"What's the problem? Did you guys have sex?"

"Yes. Several times last night," I admit.

"And now you have real feelings for her?" he asks.

"Yeah."

"And the problem is what, exactly?"

The problem is so colossal that it can't even be put into

words. What's happening between us isn't just friendship, I'm falling in love with her. The one thing I vowed I'd never do again. It almost destroyed me last time, and every fucking time I see Roxy, it's pushed into my face all over again. A constant reminder of what could have been. That can't happen with Emery. I wouldn't survive it.

"I've gotta go," I tell him.

"Hayden, don't do this—" Hudson begs, but I end the call before I can hear the rest of it.

Pacing the hotel room, I gather my stray clothes and toss them into my duffel bag. Then I pull on a T-shirt and my shoes, and I'm out the door before the shower even turns off.

My plan is to head straight for the airport and hightail it back to LA, where I can pretend like none of this ever happened. Outside the lobby of the hotel, I hail the first cab I see, tossing my duffel bag inside and then climbing in after it.

"The airport, please."

My hands are shaking as I pull out my cell phone and type out a text to Emery.

HAYDEN: Sorry. I can't do this.

Then I turn off my phone.

Chapter Eighteen

Emery

Last night was one of the best nights of my life. Being intimate with Hayden was . . . everything. It was the most incredible sex I've ever had. But the afterglow illuminated a few unpleasant things, and the stark light of morning has only confirmed them.

As I stand under the spray of warm water, lathering shampoo in my hair, I realize I can't ignore the fact that I have major feelings for him. It's kind of terrifying; sex changing our relationship is exactly what I was afraid of yesterday.

Now that the moment is here, though, I don't feel nearly as stressed as I did when I was worrying about this before. It's a fact, just as much as the sky is blue and the Sherman Act was passed in 1890 . . . I'm falling in love with Hayden Oliver. A simple truth instead of an anxious, murky possibility.

And this simple truth has a simple—although pretty

intimidating—solution. If I still want to date Hayden after we get back to Los Angeles, once I get out of the shower, we should go out for coffee and discuss it like adults. And if he doesn't return my feelings, if he wants to stay just friends . . . I think I can be a big girl about that. Probably. I just don't want to lose him and his friendship completely.

So if that's all we can have, I'll just have to adjust. Even though the thought of going without the physical part, now that I know exactly how good he is in bed—fuck, that will suck. I've never come that many times in a row before. Seriously, my body is achy in the strangest places. But the soreness in my pussy and hips is strangely pleasant, a testament to how much fun we had last night. My dry spell has sure been broken, all right, and I'm already hungry for more.

Plus I'm just plain hungry. We probably don't have time for a quickie, but I still look forward to eating breakfast with Hayden before I start my last day of boring meetings. And before our return flight, we'll have another evening all to ourselves . . .

When I come out of the bathroom, the air-conditioning

feels frigid against my damp skin, and I hug the towel tighter around me. "Lover?" I call, peeking into the living room.

It's empty. Chuckling to myself, I realize Hayden must still be in bed. Walking on air, I let the front of my towel drift open. "Up for another round already?" I call out playfully. "Or are you just a lazy . . . ?" I trail off when I realize that the bedroom is empty.

My phone vibrates, and I scurry back to the bed's nightstand to check. It's a new text from Hayden. Is he surprising me with something? The butterflies in my stomach start waking up . . .

But they fall quiet again as I read:

HAYDEN: *Sorry, I can't do this.*

So I fire back:

EMERY: Can't do what? You sprain your dick last night,
sex machine? :P Don't worry, we can find other uses
for you.

I giggle to myself and wonder seriously where he went.
To get coffee, probably.

After I've put on my business suit and makeup for the
day, there's still no answer. And when I see his things
are gone, my stomach sinks even further. Devastated, I
send another text.

EMERY: What do you mean? Where are you?

Hayden still hasn't turned up by the time I finish my
huge, lonely breakfast. The room-service bellhop
delivered enough for two people, even after I avoided
the meat stuff. I can't wait around for Hayden any
longer. I have to head downstairs for the day's first
meeting. Under the conference table, I send text after
increasingly frantic text, culminating in:

EMERY: *What the fuck are you talking about, you cryptic douche?*

No response whatsoever. Nothing but radio silence. All I can do is read and reread his original text in the hopes of deciphering something new. Five little words, as short and painful as a scalpel—aimed right where I'd just begun to heal.

I didn't think I was under any illusions. I didn't let myself dream that we might become more than friends. Hell, I probably would have been fine with fuck-buddy status. But I never imagined that Hayden would just drop everything and bail like this. Use me and then throw me away like a tissue he'd finished jerking off into. He couldn't even say good-bye to my face before he ran away. *I guess I gave him more credit than he deserves.*

Even though he probably won't answer, I still can't resist trying to call him during our lunch break. I'm not surprised when his voice-mail message immediately plays.

So this is how we end, huh? After giving me the most mind-blowing night I've ever had, he's already moved on. I almost have to laugh. Roxy was right all along; I was never anything more than his latest conquest. Considering the many years I spent in school, I feel pretty fucking stupid right now. That JD after my name doesn't mean shit. I fell for his game hook, line, and sinker.

God, I'm such an idiot—it's almost impressive how dumb I am. How many people warned me about him? Roxy got burned and tried to save me from the same fate. Mom could tell what kind of man he is with a single glance. Even his own fucking sister dropped hints that should have sent me running for the hills. They all knew better, but I was too arrogant and horny to listen to any of them. I still fell for Hayden's nice-guy act . . . playing along and dropping my panties just as he probably knew I would all along. I should have known that a shithead can't change his spots.

Have I learned nothing these past few years? My relationships with men always end in disaster. They start out hopeful, then turn into something I never signed up for. I hated the passionless sex. The dull conversations. The pretending to be interested in basketball games or whatever damn sports thing they liked to watch on TV.

But as I consider all this, I realize there was none of that with Hayden. The sex was off-the-charts hot, and I can truly say that every time he opened his mouth, he kept me entertained. There was no forcing his hobbies on me, either. He took an interest in my hobbies instead. It really felt like we were building toward something real. And then . . . *whammo*. The floor fell out from beneath me.

Hating myself almost as much as I hate Hayden, I finish my last day of business meetings in a black mood and fly home alone.

• • •

When the taxi drops me off at almost eleven, some kind of masochistic curiosity prompts me to climb past my floor and up to Hayden's. I peep around the corner of the stairwell. Light glows from underneath his condo door; he must be home for the night. I consider knocking and demanding an explanation, but right now, I'm not brave enough. The last thing I need is to break down in front of a man who's already exploited my feelings.

Besides, all my texts went unanswered and all my calls went straight to voice mail. Hayden must have turned off his phone. He's willing to miss communications from anyone, no matter how important, just to avoid even seeing my name on his screen.

So I already know perfectly well that he's pushed me away. Knocking on his door will only force me to face that rejection in person. I don't know which would be worse . . . Hayden outright sneering that he's done with me, asking why I can't take a hint, or Hayden gazing at me with pity in his eyes, trying to let me down easy. At least he won't snow me with a fake apology just to set the stage for another booty call, like my last ex would always do. Hayden's text made it pretty clear that he never wants to see me again—in or out of bed.

Lost in resentful thought, I startle when Hayden's condo door opens. I watch in horrified disbelief as a buxom, long-legged woman saunters out. She looks tired, satisfied . . . and familiar.

Is that who I think it is? Even with the building's hall lights dimmed for the night, Roxy's face is unmistakable. And she's dressed the most casual I've ever seen her, wearing flip-flops, Bermuda shorts, and a man's T-shirt . . . is it Hayden's? Her blond hair splays over her neck in a messy ponytail, as if she quickly pulled it back, and she isn't wearing any makeup. Overall, she looks like she was rode hard and put away wet.

I feel sick to my stomach. *That prick sure didn't take long to replace me, did he? And with his ex, no less.* Her dire warnings to stay away from Hayden clearly didn't apply to herself.

Before Roxy can catch me lurking—or I start crying—I duck back into the stairwell and down to the safety of my condo.

• • •

The next few days pass in a dark funk. I bitch a little to Trina over lunch, then stop when I realize it doesn't make me feel better. Neither does double-chocolate ice cream with hot fudge. Even my work can't truly distract me. I'm numb and distracted, and tired, sleeping until my alarm demands that I get up or be late for work. I skip yoga, and generally feel exhausted.

But one morning, I wake up pissed off. Not upset, not depressed, but filled with a fury that's cold and hard and strong as iron. It pushes me out of bed and into the shower like I'm preparing for battle. All my helpless self-pity has transmuted itself into determination.

No more sad-sack Emery, I decide, welcoming the cool spray on my face. No more moping and wallowing in heartbreak. I refuse to waste any more energy on that prick, not even to hate him. As Mom always says, the best revenge is living well.

I have to remind myself who I am, and the best way to do that is to get centered on my career again. I have to kick even more ass at work and double down on studying; the bar exam is only a week away now. And I have to make a clean break, so that I'm reminded of Hayden as little as possible. Which means finding a new apartment. Again.

Despite my new resolutions, I feel a residual flash of

anger at myself. What the fuck happened here? After my last boyfriend, I told everyone who would listen that I'd sworn off men, but I still managed to get tangled up with yet another jerk. I convinced myself that Hayden would be different when he was just Asshole McFuckstick: The Thrilling Sequel.

At least I got some good sex out of this whole mess, I think bitterly as I comb my hair. At least I came to my senses before he sank his claws too far into me. At least I only wasted a month of my life, instead of two years.

Even so, what's wrong with me? Am I an idiot? How many times do I have to make this kind of mistake before I learn to avoid it? Maybe I just won't have a next time at all. I should have stuck to my *no boys allowed* rule in the first place. All men ever do is confuse your priorities and fuck up your life.

I remind myself of another Mom proverb: *Spit in one hand and wish in the other, and see which one fills up first.* I can't change the past, so I force my attention back to the future and resume my pep talk.

I'm Emery Winters, damn it, I repeat silently while I get

239 • *Screwed*

dressed and put on my makeup. I don't need men. I don't need anyone. I'm a lean, mean legal machine. I eat textbooks for breakfast and contracts for dessert. No one can fuck with me.

Speaking of which . . . I tell my growling stomach to hold its horses. There's something I have to take care of before work, and I don't want to be late. Besides, it's Monday, so there will be free donuts in the conference room. *Think of the sprinkles. No, wait, don't think of them yet.*

At last, I look as fierce and polished as I wish I felt. I dig my tenant agreement out of my filing cabinet and head downstairs to the building manager's office.

"Good morning," I say as I walk up to his desk, aiming for a tone that's cheerful yet brisk. "I'd like to inquire about canceling my lease on 4B."

The small, skinny man takes the heavy packet and turns to its last page. He blinks slowly as he reads, like an old owl. "This is a twelve-month lease," he finally says. "You've only lived here for . . . six weeks?"

"Yes, I know. I'm willing to pay the fee for early cancellation." I pull my checkbook out of my purse. "I can write you a check now if you want."

Another long blink. "Is there something wrong with your unit?"

Yeah, your boss's dick got into it. "Not at all. It's a great place," I say with a smile. "I just need to move." And this guy just needs to stop grilling me and fill out the paperwork already.

"I see," he replies, looking like he doesn't see at all. "Hold on a moment, ma'am. Let me check with Mr. Oliver."

Oh, for fuck's sake. I wait as patiently as I can while he dials and mutters into the phone. After five minutes that feel like five hours, he hangs up. "He'll be right with you."

"Uh . . . sure."

With a heroic effort, I maintain my smile while screaming internally. This is absolutely the last thing I wanted. I'm not ready to see him face-to-face yet. But here he comes . . . After what feels like only a split second, I hear footsteps coming down the hallway. The familiar sound of his leather dress loafers on carpet.

When Hayden walks in, time screeches to a halt. My empty stomach constricts at the sight of him. All the hurt and betrayal I felt in Omaha comes flooding back with a motherfucking vengeance. It took me days before I could even start moving on—but this bastard never had anything to move on from. He played me like a violin, got what he wanted from me, and then hooked up with his ex the very next night.

And he looks as delicious as ever. That just adds insult to injury. He stomped my heart into the dirt and my body still wants a piece of him. Everything about this is so incredibly unfair. I try to grasp that anger, draw on it, and let it strengthen my resolve again.

Hayden's expression seems kind of pissed off too. As soon as his blue eyes meet mine, though, his irritation fades into what looks almost like regret. "You want to move?" he asks.

What I want is to spit a defiant *yes* at him and swish out of here like a diva. He didn't ask why I'm canceling my lease; he knows damn well what this is about. But I'm suddenly not sure if I can trust my voice, so instead, I just nod at him.

"Okay," Hayden replies in a carefully neutral tone that I can't read. He turns to the building manager. "Go ahead and cancel Miss Winters's lease. No penalty."

And with that, he walks out the office door, leaving both of us speechless. Hayden still seems pretty upset under his flat, even facade. But not at me.

At himself? Why, when he was the one who tossed me aside in the first place?

I hesitate, anxiety warring with curiosity, and anger playing both sides of the field. Then I shake my head and stomp after Hayden. It's time for me to get back to work . . . but before I can do that, I need to lay this mystery to rest. Or else it will never leave me alone.

Chapter Nineteen

Hayden

It's been several days since I saw Emery, and my heart beats wildly in my chest as I watch her approach. She's in one of her trademark fitted dark suit jackets and pencil skirts, and she looks beautiful, smart, and put together. It makes me miss her even more. Her heels click loudly across the sidewalk as she moves with purpose toward me.

"Do you have anything to say for yourself?" she asks, venom in her tone. If she was subdued in the leasing office, now she's full of fire.

A stabbing pain flares in my chest when our eyes connect. "That I'm an asshole, and you were right all along." The words come from someplace deep inside me, so I know they're true.

"You just up and leave me in a hotel room in Nebraska, turn off your phone and, what . . . start fucking Roxy? Just for fun? Just to see if you could royally fuck me over like everyone warned me about?" Her voice is loud and angry, but her eyes well with tears at those last words.

"You don't know anything about me and Roxy."

Her eyes widen and her nostrils flare. "No. You're right. I don't. Because you never told me anything about you and Roxy! I opened up to you so many times, and you couldn't do the same."

Glancing around, I see a few of the nosier tenants have gathered on the sidewalk and are watching our spectacle.

"Come with me. There's something I need to tell you."

She narrows her eyes, and for a second I think she's going to refuse me. But then I say, "Please," and her gaze softens. She might not want to hear my explanation, but something in her *needs* to hear it. Closure, I'm guessing.

"Okay." Her tone is defeated, and I hate that. Her usual spark has faded, and everything in me wants to fix it. Part of me wants her to yell and scream and hit me, but she doesn't, even though I deserve that and more.

She follows me upstairs to my place, and when we enter, I can hear Dottie humming from the other room. I forgot she was here. One sighting of Emery and my head went completely blank, I guess.

Dottie pokes her head out from my bedroom. "Hi, boss. Didn't know you'd be back this morning."

"Dottie, could you excuse us, please?"

Her brows pinch together as she glances between me and Emery. Emery is visibly upset, with her hands balled up tightly by her sides and her face red.

"Sure," Dottie says slowly.

"You can take the rest of the day off. Paid. Take your grandson to the beach or something," I suggest.

She nods, and scurries out the door moments later.

Then it's just the two of us left alone in my condo. Bright sunlight streams in through the windows, and it's too quiet.

"You're going to move out?" I ask.

"What did you expect me to do, Hayden? Continue

living here where I have to see you every day? No thanks. I have more respect for myself than that." She plants her hands on her hips. "But I didn't come up here to explain myself to you. You said you had something you needed to tell me."

"Right." I nod. "Please come sit down."

We go into the living room and Emery takes a seat on the couch, her posture as straight as an arrow. She watches me warily. I wonder if the real reason she wants to move out is because being near me is painful to her, which would mean she has feelings for me. Or maybe it's just that she's pissed off and hates my guts. Either way, I have to take a chance.

"This isn't easy for me, but there are some things I need to get off my chest."

She crosses her arms in front of her. "Fine. I'm listening."

"Roxy and I have a past." *Fucking understatement of the year.*

"No shit," she mutters under her breath. "You think

I've just now figured that out? I saw her sneak out of your place late the other night—just after we had been together. She ducked out of here so fast, clearly doing the walk of shame." She rolls her eyes for dramatic effect.

"That night, I asked her to come over to set things right between us. Nothing happened, if that's what you're implying. I haven't slept with anyone else since you."

"And you just expect me to believe you? Take that at face value?"

"I'm an asshole and an idiot, but I'm not a liar. I've never once lied to you."

She works her bottom lip between her teeth.

"I have to start at the beginning, or I won't get this right." Rubbing one hand over the back of my neck, I take a deep breath. "Her real name is Naomi. Roxy's just a stage name. I knew her before she was Roxy, long before she was a stripper. We met in college. She was a dance major, believe it or not."

I look up to see Emery's reaction. Her mouth is hanging open.

"We dated for three years. I was crazy about her. I loved her free spirit, her straightforward outlook on life. She always seemed wise beyond her years, nothing like the bubblegum-chewing sorority girls who would give me doe eyes and then whine when I didn't ask them out. Naomi was confident. Fun. She didn't need a man. It made me want to be around her even more. Honestly, the way she was back then . . . kind of reminds me of you."

I meant it as a compliment, but I have no idea if Emery takes it that way. Her expression remains impassive as she waits for me to continue.

"Our junior year, she broke her ankle in three places in a bad roller-blading accident, and had to have a couple of surgeries. It ended up costing her the dance scholarship that paid for her college, and she eventually dropped out of school. Things changed between us after that. She became . . . resentful, even though I tried to be as supportive as I could. I even had her move in with me, because she needed extra help getting around while she was recovering. But being together twenty-four/seven only seemed to make things worse between us."

I take a deep breath, knowing this next part of the story isn't going to be pretty.

"A few months later, Naomi told me she was pregnant. I was over-the-moon happy. I figured it was exactly what we both needed—I thought it would get our relationship back on track and give her something positive in her life to focus on, since her dance career had been effectively ruined. And even though I was young, I was excited about the baby. I bought all the books on parenting, and little rattles and blankets. It was nuts, but it was the only positive thing in my life at that time."

Emery leans forward, her fingertips on her lips.

"She hated that I was happy about that baby. She said she didn't know if she ever wanted kids, and certainly not when we were just twenty years old. It drove an even bigger wedge between us. And then . . ." I blow out a big breath I didn't know I was holding. "Two weeks later, she told me that she'd lost the baby—had a miscarriage. Part of me didn't believe her. Knowing how she felt about the pregnancy, I didn't put it past her to just go off and have an abortion without telling me."

A lump forms in my throat, and I have to take a minute to collect myself. In my mind, I see a life that could have been, but never was. A little boy with my dark hair and her brown eyes toddling along beside me. I can see it so clearly, and it cuts like a knife through me. As he grew, I would show him everything I knew, all the ways to be a man. I'd take him with me to the properties we were renovating, let him help as much as he wanted. A paintbrush in his chubby fingers by the age of four. He'd learn responsibility, and I wouldn't have to miss a minute of watching him grow. Working alongside me, he could learn a trade if he was the type who wanted to work with his hands, or if he preferred to be behind the scenes like me, I'd show him the finance side of things.

"Oh my God." Emery's eyes are wide and her hands are clenched in her lap. "Do you really think . . . ?"

Blinking away the mirage, I shrug. "Not anymore. That night you saw her leaving my place, I was so fucking confused about you, and I . . . I asked her to come over. I felt like I couldn't face our future if I didn't really have closure on my past."

Emery's nose twitches at that phrase—*our future*—but she doesn't probe me on it. "What did she say?"

"We talked about everything—things that we hadn't brought up in years. She handed me a piece of paper from her doctor, showing that she'd been diagnosed as having a miscarriage all those years ago. She'd been telling the truth the whole time."

"I'm sorry," Emery says quietly.

"A baby between us wouldn't have solved the huge rifts in our relationship. I see that now. And I realize that blaming her for how things turned out between us wasn't fair. But it's in the past, I guess, right?"

She nods, her expression softening.

"My point is, losing her, losing our baby . . . it fucked me up. It made me turn into a guy I didn't even like. But I had to protect my heart. I couldn't get involved in anything serious again. My mission in life became all about having fun and living in the moment with no regrets. Kids were no longer on my radar, and a serious relationship was the last thing I wanted."

"I get it, Hayden," she says. "But why do you call her

Roxy, and not Naomi?"

I shrug. "To me, the person she is now . . . she's Roxy. Naomi, that girl I fell in love with all those years ago, is gone. It was tragic what happened to her, but I know she's moved on. She's happy with her life. She isn't one of those poor, helpless girls stuck in a degrading job. She actually loves stripping, loves what she does. And honestly, it's a classy club."

"You've been there to see her dance?" Emery's voice rises in confusion.

"No. I went there once a long time ago for a bachelor party, so I'm familiar with the place. That's all I meant. Watching Roxy dance would be too weird."

"Yeah, I guess so." Emery rises to her feet. "Well, thanks for explaining all of that to me. I guess it does clear some things up. But I've got a lot of packing to do, so I should be going."

"I'm not nearly done explaining anything to you."

Confusion settles over her features, etching a line between her brows. "You're not?"

"Please sit back down."

Bending her knees, she lowers herself to the couch once again. And I take another deep breath, ready to peel back another layer and expose myself to her.

"That morning in Omaha, after the best sex of my life . . ." Her eyes widen. "You farted."

"God, Hayden. I know, I'm sorry. I'm a disgusting creature. I get it." She throws her hands up in the air. "For fuck's sake—grow up."

"No, just listen." I clear my throat. "In my world, women didn't pass gas, they didn't belch, or shit, or do any of that other disgusting stuff men do."

She rolls her eyes.

"But then you did that and I thought it was cute. Like, legitimately. I wasn't grossed out; I wasn't disgusted. I actually liked the fact that you were comfortable enough around me to let go and be yourself."

She tosses a throw pillow at me, but there's a smirk on her mouth. "I told you, that was an accident. It had nothing to do with being *comfortable*."

"I know. But it made me realize just how deep my feelings for you ran. I was willing to throw all my rules out the window. I was a different person with you. That scared me. And you're so driven with your career, and not looking for a man, that scared me too. I thought it'd be history repeating itself all over again."

"And you ran." Disappointment flashes in her eyes.

I don't know why I thought explaining all of this would automatically entitle me to forgiveness. Of course it doesn't work that way. Emery's been hurt by the men in her past too many times.

"You have to understand," I tell her. "I've been haunted for a long time, thinking I was cursed when it came to love. Feeling what I did for you has only dredged up all those old feelings of confusion and heartache and abandonment."

"I wish you could have explained that to me before just completely shutting me out. That was really shitty of you." She looks down at her hands as she says this, and I can't help moving over to sit beside her on the couch.

"I'm sorry I left that morning. I'm sorry about everything. I should have told you about Naomi sooner."

I take her hand in mine, and Emery gazes up at me. "Did you mean everything you said . . . about me being the best sex of your life, and about you being different with me?"

"Every word. I hope you believe that. Can you forgive me for running out?" I'm pleading with her, my voice solemn and serious.

She nods. "Yeah. I always knew you were a dipshit, but I also believe there's hope for you yet." There are tears shimmering in her eyes as she says this, as if she doesn't quite know if she can let herself believe it yet. "I've missed you, our friendship," she says.

"I've missed more than that," I admit.

"Me too," she adds softly. "But I know you don't do relationships." Her voice is sad.

"I'm trainable. Entirely." I rub careful circles over the back of her hand.

"We'll see about that."

A tiny flicker of that spark I fell for is back, and I breathe just a little easier. Then Emery jumps to her feet again, looking panicked. "Shit. What time is it? I'm going to be late for work."

A quick glance at the wall clock shows it's almost eight, and my gut cramps at the thought of her leaving. "Call in sick. Spend the day with me." I'm pretty sure I've never once muttered that phrase in my life, and once it's out of my mouth, it's further proof that this woman does strange things to me.

She's silent for several moments, leaving me terrified that she'll reject me. She takes a deep breath and I think she's going to blow me off, tell me that she can't. But then she straightens her shoulders and looks me in the eye. "If I do that, you're going to spend every second of today groveling . . . and I need to study."

I nod, suddenly eager to please. "Absolutely. You can study, and I'll even go out and pick up lunch later."

A small smile adorns her lips, and she digs her phone

out of her purse and begins typing a message—which I assume is an e-mail to tell her boss she won't be in today.

"The lunch will be of my choosing. Correct?" she asks, glancing up at me as she taps out the rest of her message and then shoves her phone back in her purse.

"Of course. Anything you want. But first . . ."

"What?" she asks.

"I'm going to kiss you."

Unable to resist, I cross the room in two long strides and pull her into my arms, her chest bumping against mine. She releases a surprised gasp. Then my lips crash down on hers and she opens for me, letting my tongue invade her mouth in a passionate kiss. With our mouths fused together in hungry kisses, my hands wander down to squeeze her ass. Emery groans into my mouth, and I know she wants this every bit as much as I do. Even if we don't quite know where we stand, even if our future is still murky, even if she hasn't completely forgiven me yet. She and I both know how perfectly we fit together.

"Let me take you to bed."

She breaks from the kiss, her eyes on mine reflecting so much emotion—past heartbreak and confusion, but underneath it all, lust.

"I'm not going anywhere. I swear this time. I just want to make you feel good." It's the only way I know how to fix this. I don't want to get off—I want intimacy and physical closeness with her.

She nods and lets me guide her into my bedroom.

As I take my time slowly stripping her from her dressy work clothes, one thing strikes me. It's Dottie's wisdom from weeks ago—that nice girls don't wear the kind of panties she'd found under my bed. I think Dottie would be pleased to know that Emery's wearing white cotton, no-nonsense granny panties. And she's still the hottest fucking thing I've ever seen. If Dottie's right about this, and she usually is, then Emery is a keeper. And viewing her as wife material doesn't make me want to run. It makes me want to keep her all to myself. For always.

We fall into bed, my lips at her throat, her hands on my cock, my fingers inside her panties . . . and while our movements are hungry, nothing about this is rushed.

We take our time exploring each other's bodies, stroking, kissing, murmuring encouraging things about how good it all feels.

As I slowly enter her, her breathing hitches and her eyes never leave mine. "We fit together perfectly," I say, kissing her parted lips.

"So perfect," she cries, tilting her pelvis up to take me deeper.

Soon I can't hold back, and I'm pounding into her body again and again while she makes little mewling cries of pleasure. And while I still wonder what's next for us, I push those thoughts away and lose myself in the pleasure of her body, taking all she's offering and giving all I have in return.

After we make love twice more, I go into the kitchen to make us a snack while Emery naps. If she's serious about getting some studying done today—and I know she is—she'll need some brain fuel. I start a pot of coffee and fry up a couple of eggs. When I peek back into the bedroom, I love the way she looks in my bed. Dark hair spread out over my pillow, her rounded hips draped with the sheet.

As I watch her while she sleeps, I can't help the tender thoughts floating through my brain about how close I came to losing her . . . and how lucky I am that I didn't.

Now I just have to do my best not to fuck this up.

Chapter Twenty

Emery

Surrounded by teetering stacks of class notes and thick textbooks splayed open on their spines, I sit cross-legged on the living room floor. I started studying on the dining table, then moved to the bed when I ran out of territory to spread out in. Then I shoved the coffee table outside on the balcony, tossed down a couch cushion, and turned the entire floor into my desk.

Now I'm curled up at the center of a paper-and-pillow nest. My back is killing me, my eyes feel gritty, my tongue tastes sour from too much coffee, and . . . my ass is vibrating?

I thought I left my phone on its charger, but when I dig in my shorts pocket, there it is. And I have a text from Hayden.

HAYDEN: You still up? Wanna make a taco run?

I pat my hollow stomach, trying to remember the last time I ate. Probably my dinner break at work. And it's midnight now, which means . . . how many hours ago? My brain has no room left for basic math anymore. I've crammed it too full of legal definitions and case histories.

My groggy attempt at thought is interrupted by a second text.

HAYDEN: Or would you rather I taste your taco? ;)

Oh, for fuck's sake. I snort in half amusement, half exasperation and text him back.

EMERY: Seriously? Are you twelve years old?

HAYDEN: I hope not, or you might get arrested.

I tried going to work on two hours yesterday. It didn't end well.

Speaking of stuff I don't have time for, I should stop texting Hayden. I stand up and barely catch myself before I stumble. *Whoa . . . head rush.* I must have gotten up too fast. I blink the blurriness out of my vision and stretch my stiff muscles. Then I pick my way through the minefield of paper and put my phone back on my nightstand where it belongs.

Just as I get settled again, someone knocks at the door. I groan and drag myself across the condo to look through the peephole. It's Hayden, holding a brown paper box labeled TACO FARM: ONE DOZEN FRESH under his arm.

Wow, that was quick. I glance at the clock. Wait, no . . . it's been half an hour. I've just lost all ability to keep track of time. Terrific.

I open the door and sigh. "I said no tacos. That includes coming over, not just going out."

"You have to eat sometime. I won't hang around too long, I promise." He looks over my shoulder into the condo. "Holy shit, what happened here? Did a library explode?"

"No, just my brain."

He makes a sympathetic noise. "So are you going to let me in or what?"

I give up and stand aside. Maybe some food will help me find my second wind . . . and even though things are still a little uncertain between us, I miss Hayden. I haven't had much time to spend with him over the past few days. Not after that day I skipped work and we had mind-blowing sex all afternoon.

As he gets out plates and arranges our midnight snack on the dining table, he asks, "Anything I can help with?"

"Not unless you're secretly an expert in dignitary tort law. But thanks for the offer . . . and the food." My stomach is already perking up at the smell of spicy tempeh and grilled vegetables.

"I have no idea what the fuck that is. Something about serious cakes?" He returns my tired smile. "And you're welcome."

We sit down to inhale our second dinner. Before I know it, I've polished off all six of the delicious little bastards. I lie back in my chair, feeling fat and happy. My blood sugar is singing my praises. This little break definitely helped. But Hayden looks more pensive than satisfied, and he's left two of his steak tacos uneaten.

"Penny for your thoughts," I say.

He blinks. "Huh? Why do you ask?"

I point at his half-full plate. "I know you. When you don't finish your dead cow, it's gotta be serious."

"Okay, fine. I did want to ask you something." He chews his lip for a second. "Are you still going to move out?"

Now it's my turn to blink at him. The possibility hadn't even occurred to me. I only wanted to move out in the first place because I thought that Hayden had returned to his old asshole ways. When I found out why he left me in Omaha and why Roxy was in his condo so late, I realized that Hayden has always been my friend. He just panicked and acted like an idiot. Not like I've never done that before.

With that issue out of the way, though, I'm left with my original problem: how to handle my own feelings for him. On that day when Hayden bared all his scars to me, so open and brave, I let my pussy call the shots. Once again, I fell into his bed without knowing or caring what it meant in the long run. But I have to make our relationship crystal clear—to both of us—before we end up tripping and falling on top of each other again. Does he still think of me as a friend with benefits? And would I be happy in that arrangement?

I shake my head. "No, I'm staying here," I reply. "I already went to the building manager and told him to forget about my termination request. But I do want to know . . . where we stand."

He takes a deep, slow breath through his nose. "You mean, are we dating?"

"Yes. And are we exclusive?" I study his face for any trace of expression, any hint about what's going through his mind right now.

After a minute, Hayden nods thoughtfully. "I can do that," he says in the same tone he agreed to trying yoga, when we first met in June. Barely two months ago—and yet it feels like we've known each other for years.

I raise my eyebrows in an urgent stare. "Are you sure? Don't say yes just to avoid hurting my feelings. I need to know what you really want, not just what you think I want to hear."

He reaches over the table to take my hands in his. My heart flutters at what I glimpse in his sea-blue eyes. The honesty, the vulnerability, the pure need . . . the love.

"What I want is you," he replies, before pulling me into a hot, tender kiss.

Chapter Twenty-One

Emery

Leaning into the mirror, I dab on my last swipes of eye shadow, careful not to let any powder fall onto my red satin cocktail dress. I love that I can dress for a five-star restaurant without freezing to death; my first autumn in Los Angeles feels like a Michigan summer. I guess that's a fair trade for the hellish weather I endured when I first arrived.

Just as I finish my makeup, there's a knock at the door. I put down my brush and hurry out of the bathroom to answer.

It's Hayden, right on time and looking absolutely mouthwatering in a tailored gray suit. He gives me a slow, burning glance from head to toe that tells me he likes what he sees. "On second thought, we don't have to go out tonight. Want to just stay home?"

"You mean stay in bed," I retort, matching his crooked grin.

"What? I didn't say that." He puts on a faux innocent look, but he can't stop the corners of his mouth from twitching. "You have a dirty mind, Miss Winters."

I swat his arm gently. "You forgetting something? I've passed the bar and been sworn in. Now I'm Miss Emery Winters, *Esquire*. And nothing can stop me from going out to celebrate."

"All right, all right . . . your wish is my command. I'll wait." He leans in to kiss me on the neck, knowing to avoid my fresh makeup without being told. It's barely a brush of lips, so soft, almost chaste, but it still gives me a little shiver. His husky murmur catches me off guard. "But I'll be counting the seconds until I can peel you out of that dress."

Patience suddenly doesn't seem like much of a virtue. But I know from experience that anticipation makes things so much sweeter. "Don't get too excited, horn-dog," I say, trying to sound stern instead of turned on. "We wouldn't want to get thrown out of the restaurant."

"If I'm a dog, then isn't it my master's fault if I don't behave?" Hayden offers his elbow before I can come up with a snappy retort. "Come on, let's go. Our reservation is in forty-five minutes, and rush hour isn't over yet."

"Are you serious?" I glance at the clock. "It's after eight."

"It's also Friday night in downtown LA." He escorts me downstairs like I'm a princess and opens the door of his BMW for me.

We make good time and arrive ten minutes early. The restaurant is gorgeous with dark wood paneling, crystal chandeliers, white-draped tables with lilies almost as bright as the candles they're arranged under. After the hostess seats us at a small table for two, I twist around to admire the view until I notice Hayden smiling at me.

"What?" I ask defensively. "It's a nice place."

I expect him to tease me—to say something like *I thought your head was going to fall off* or *Were you looking for the tofu?* But he simply replies, "You're beautiful."

My cheeks heat up with sudden shyness. Love shines from his eyes, so naked and tender that I swallow hard, fighting back happy tears. Before I can figure out how to reply, the waiter chooses that moment to deliver the menus. Hayden orders his customary Scotch, I order an appletini, and the waiter flits away to let us decide on our entrees.

"You know . . . I actually have something else to celebrate," I say between sips. "I didn't get a chance to tell you before."

"More good news? Jeez, leave some for the rest of us." His grin is bursting with pride. "So? What is it?"

"I've been promoted. Well, technically *hired*, but same diff. Walker, Price, and Pratt made me a junior associate yesterday."

Hayden blinks at me. Then he stands up, pushes aside the table's centerpiece, and leans over the table to press a fiery kiss to my mouth, lipstick be damned. My hands flutter at his shoulders, wanting to pull him closer, but too aware of how many people can see us. I finally muster the willpower to push him away when an old couple at a nearby table start clapping.

"Oh my God, sit down." I bury my burning face in my

hands. "They probably think you just proposed or something."

"Screw them. Let them think whatever they want . . . this is great news, baby." But he does sit back down when the waiter reappears.

After we've given our orders, Hayden picks up where he left off. "So now that you're a card-carrying lawyer, is that asshole finally going to give you some respect?"

"You mean Mr. Pratt? I doubt it . . . creepers gonna creep," I say with a shrug. "But I've got things under control. Whenever I need to cool his jets, I just casually mention my boyfriend. That works pretty well."

"Ah, yes. Your overprotective boyfriend who might just punch him so hard, his bad hair plugs fall out." Hayden rubs his chin. "I wonder if he lives in a building I own . . ."

I giggle despite myself. "Easy there, Rambo. I handled him just fine before we started dating. And if I perform well enough to get a good letter of recommendation, Trina might be able to hook me up at her new job next year. So I don't need you stirring shit. Okay?"

He holds up his hands in surrender. "Fair enough. Shit will be shaken, not stirred."

"Ew, gross." I make a face. "I'm trying to eat here."

"No, you're not. You're drinking that . . . neon-green thing. Christ, just looking at it makes me feel like less of a man."

Sticking my tongue out at him, I toe off one high heel under the table. He sucks in his breath when I slide my foot up his thigh. "Does this help? I think I feel your masculinity coming back . . ."

"Oh, you are going to *get* it later," he growls with a wicked smirk.

Heat boils in my belly as I flash my own faux-sweet smile. "I'll hold you to that."

Our veal marsala and eggplant parmesan land in front of us, and we dig in eagerly. I don't know about Hayden, but I'm starved. I worked through my usual dinner break so I could come home early and primp for our date. For a few minutes, we just enjoy the gourmet

Italian cuisine in blissful silence.

"I didn't tell you the best part yet," I say after I've shut up my stomach. "As a junior associate, my salary will be almost twice as much as I made when I was an intern. And that'll only go up with seniority. Mom should be able to retire within three years . . . five at the outside."

"Five freaking years? Isn't she already sixty-three?" His mouth twists in uncertainty. "You know, I can still start an account for her. Under both your names, so I can't touch it after I make the initial deposit."

I shake my head, smiling at him. "Thanks, sweetie, but I'm never going to change my answer. I can do this standing on my own two feet." No matter how many times he offers money, all I want from Hayden is his love—and he's made it clear that I have it in spades. "Besides, I still have to *convince* Mom to retire. She'll probably say something like"—I lower my voice in imitation of her—"I'll go stir-crazy doing nothing all day! I won't sponge off my own daughter just so I can sit on my heinie."

He lets out a bark of laughter. "That sounds like Val, all

right. She's a real—"

"Stubborn battle-ax?"

"I was going to say 'a real independent lady.' But you know, I think she'd take 'stubborn battle-ax' as a compliment."

"She probably would." I chuckle affectionately.

"So now that you've got the perfect degree, the perfect job, and the perfect boyfriend . . ." He bounces his eyebrows until I snort at him. "What's next on the world-domination agenda?"

"If I have the perfect boyfriend, then you tell me?" I ask. "I still wonder how I could ever compete with Roxy. Being sexy is literally her job."

My tone is joking, but Hayden fixes me with a solemn look. "You don't have to. Naomi and I had a good run, but it ended years ago. She's enjoying the single life now . . . and I've found what I was looking for all along." He takes my hand, his expression softening into adoration. "I love you, Emery. So much."

Emotion knots in my throat. "I . . . I love you too," I

stammer, smiling and blinking back tears for the second time tonight. I'm still so new to those three little words—both hearing and saying them—that they touch my heart every time. But the mood has become way too serious for what's supposed to be a celebration. So I rub his knuckles with my thumb and purr, "Still, I'm sure she must have taught you a few things. Why don't we go back to your place and practice?"

Understanding dawns on his face and he grins, suddenly all mischief again. "Excuse me," Hayden calls out. "Can we get the check?"

The waiter hustles over. "No dessert this evening, sir?"

"We'll be having dessert at home," I interrupt smoothly.

The waiter nods and leaves, and Hayden winks at me. I roll my eyes with a chuckle.

• • •

We barely get through Hayden's door before we're glued to each other, making out like teenagers. I nip his lower lip, then draw back when he makes a brief, husky noise. "Go sit down," I order. "There's something I want to do."

"Well, well. Someone's feeling bossy tonight." Despite his back talk, he's already walking over to the couch.

I raise one eyebrow. "Will that be a problem?"

He grins. "Not at all, ma'am."

Letting my hips sway, I stroll to a spot just out of his reach. Under his appreciative eyes, I reach back and undo my zipper, pulling it down slowly. I slide the gown's straps over my shoulders to reveal first my cleavage, then my lacy black bra. He watches with a wolfish smile and tented pants as I finally let the silky material pool around my feet.

"Damn . . . I didn't know you'd be wearing a thong," he purrs.

"If I told you, we never would have made it to the restaurant." I step out of the gown, now standing in only my lingerie, jewelry, and shoes. "Should I leave my heels on?"

He leans forward to caress me, watching his hands slide

down over the curve from waist to hip to thigh. The tip of his tongue flickers over his lips, as if imagining how I taste, and I shiver at the sight as much as his touch.

"Damn, woman, you're asking me to make a decision right now? There's no blood left in my brain."

"I didn't know you ever had blood in your brain."

With a playful growl, he lunges forward to squeeze my ass. Startled, I squeak . . . then moan when he seals his mouth around my nipple. His gentle teeth and nimble tongue tease the pebbled nub right through the lace, sparking pleasure straight through me, as if his mouth were on my clit instead.

"Cheater." I sigh, swaying on my feet. "You were supposed to wait until the end of the strip show."

"I've been waiting all night." He sucks hard and I almost whimper. "Hell, I've been waiting all week. I want to make you come."

"Not yet, big boy," I tease. That little declaration takes every ounce of restraint I have. Because Hayden knows how to dole out the O's like nobody's business.

I ease down onto my knees in front of him, blinking up at him innocently through my eyelashes as I slowly tug down his zipper and reach inside his boxers to free the heavy weight of his cock. He feels so good in my palm, thick and hot and hard. But I know he'll feel even better in my mouth. This is something I haven't gotten the chance to do yet.

Over the last couple of days, we both had the chance to get tested and sort out birth control, so now, tonight will be the first time we make love bare. I can hardly wait, but I want to take him with my mouth first. Holding the base of him steady with both hands, I lower my head to his lap.

"Emery, you don't have to . . . *Fuuuuuuck.*" Hayden curses when my tongue makes contact, licking up the length of him like he's my own personal lollipop.

"Don't have to what?" I purr, my tongue teasing the top of him.

"Shit. Do that again."

He pushes my hair back from my face and lightly cups my jaw in his large palms. I feel the love, adoration, and desire rolling off of him in waves. It only makes me want him more.

I open wide and take in as much of him as I can. Hayden's hips rock up in gentle thrusts as my mouth moves over him. My hand slides over him as I suck. Up and down. Up and down.

"Baby," he says on a grunt, his hand tightening at the back of my neck. "Come here."

I let him pull me up off the floor to straddle his lap. His erection strains against me, hot and eager. I pull my panties aside—I've been soaking wet for hours—and rock my hips, feeling how much he wants me back.

"Emery . . ." He pants, grinding back up into me. "Jesus, you're so . . ." At a loss for words, he pulls me into a hungry kiss and rocks his cock against my folds.

No more waiting. I need him now. I sink down onto his cock inch by inch, as fast as I can take it. The hot fullness as he pushes inside me—almost pain, but definitely not—takes my breath away. He's so thick and long, stretching me, rubbing against every sensitive spot.

We've barely moved and I'm already panting.

Then he snaps his hips up hard, pounding right into the best spot of all, and I damn near scream. "Fuck!"

"That is, in fact, what we're doing," he says with a chuckle.

How can the man wisecrack at a time like this? I guess that's one of the many reasons I love Hayden . . . which all too often overlap with reasons I want to slap him.

"Then stop talking about it and do it," I gasp.

When he starts thrusting in earnest, another cry tears itself from my throat. I brace myself on his shoulders, slamming my hips up and down, still barely able to keep up. He groans into my mouth and I can feel his adoring smile against my lips. He's just as swept up as I am, just as overwhelmed by love and lust.

When I first arrived in this new life, I was warned that this silly, cute, cocky, infuriating man was my enemy. I became his friend instead. And now . . . he's just plain mine.

Epilogue

Hayden

Emery and I are seated across the dining room table from Beth and David. Gracie sits beside me. The kids have been put to bed, and the dinner dishes sit undone on the kitchen island.

It was an amazing sight to watch Beth and Emery cook together in the kitchen, preparing two versions of the paella we had tonight—one vegetarian and one regular. Gracie even joined Emery in eating the vegetarian option. A move of solidarity or something. It's cool both of my sisters are accepting her. But why wouldn't they? She's smart, funny, and all around a cool person.

My hand finds Emery's under the table, and I give it a squeeze. She looks over at me with a healthy glow on her cheeks and love radiating from her eyes. I've told both my sisters privately, as well as Hudson, that I was in love with Emery, and after the initial shock, they were thrilled for me. For us.

Gracie leans forward, putting her elbows on the table. "You guys are so cute together." She's always been a romantic, my little sister, even though she's never had a serious boyfriend. "Hayden, when did you first know you were in love with Emery?" she asks.

Emery's gaze snaps to mine and her smile fades. "Don't you dare answer that."

A smile quirks up my lips. "It was in our hotel room in Omaha."

A sharp jab to my ribs steals my breath. "Seriously, I'm warning you," she says.

"Emery did this really *cute* thing in the morning, and I knew right then." I grin at her.

She rolls her eyes, but her expression is playful. "And then your jackass brother got scared and ran."

Beth and Gracie both make grunting noises of disgust. But they know this story; they know I groveled my way back into her good graces. I'm done running.

"Are you mad?" I lean over and whisper to Emery.

She leans close to my ear, so only I can hear, and

whispers. "You have a nine-inch cock, and you know where the G-spot is. I love the fuck out of you, flaws and all."

And just like that, my heart soars. Her love feels so good. Like *putting on your favorite T-shirt and lying in bed all day watching funny movies* good.

"I love you too," I whisper back, kissing her forehead. I am so in love, and so fucking proud of my sexy, kick-ass girlfriend.

I lean in close again and tease her by making a quiet farting sound into her ear. She punches me in the arm, but we're both grinning like love-struck fools.

"You're screwed later," she teases right back, narrowing her eyes.

"Promise?" I ask, giving her a flirty wink.

A deep, throaty laugh tumbles from her mouth, and Emery slaps a hand over it. I squeeze her knee under the table, unable to keep my greedy hands to myself.

It's weird how easily she fits into my life. Hudson loves

her. She and Roxy are still good friends, and now it's obvious that my sisters love her too. There's no way I'm letting her go . . . after all, I'll never find another girl with cuter farts.

Monster Prick

A Screwed spin-off novella

Over my dead body.

That's what I told Gracie when she informed me of her plan to pick some random guy she met online to get rid of her pesky virginity.

If anyone is touching her, it's going to be me.

I shouldn't even be considering it, but I can't get it out of my head—her under me, begging me.

• • •

Arrogant. Cocky. Prick.

Those are the words I'd use to describe my older brother's dangerously handsome best friend.

When he learned of my plan to kick off my white cotton briefs, ditching my good-girl persona once and for all by losing my virginity to the first eligible bachelor I could find, he flipped out. Said over his dead body.

He says if anyone's going to do it, it's going to be him.

I hate that I'm even considering his offer. But I am . . . I *sooo* am.

Ever since he suggested it, all I can think about is his cocky smile on those full lips as he's driving into me.

But if we cross that line . . . will I ever be able to go back?

Acknowledgments

A hearty thank-you to Pam Berehulke, Danielle Sanchez, Angela Smith, and Rachel Brookes. You each play a significant role in helping me on my writing journey. Each novel is different, some more difficult than others, so thank you for being there to support me.

To all of the bloggers, fans, and readers who have shared my books with others, who've left reviews and made beautiful graphic teasers, my heart is filled with bookish love for you. I hope you know how critical you are to this community. I'm grateful for every tweet, review, and mention. My readers mean everything to me, and I'm blessed to have your support.

To my little family. You're everything to me.

About the Author

A *New York Times*, *Wall Street Journal*, and *USA Today* best-selling author of more than eighteen titles, Kendall Ryan has sold more than a million e-books, and her books have been translated into several languages in countries around the world. She's a traditionally published author with Simon & Schuster and Harper Collins UK, as well as enjoying success as an independently published author. Since she first began self-publishing in 2012, she's appeared at #1 on Barnes & Noble and iBooks charts around the world. Her books have also appeared on the *New York Times* and *USA Today* best-seller list twenty-three times.

Website: www.kendallryanbooks.com

Facebook: Kendall Ryan Books

Twitter: @kendallryan1

Instagram: www.instagram.com/kendallryan1

Other Books by Kendall Ryan

CPSIA information can be obtained at www.ICGtesting.com
Printed in the USA
BVOW02s0601280716

457065BV00008B/262/P